Counsellor
Acquisition Series Book 1

Celia Aaron

Counsellor

Acquisition Series, Book 1

Celia Aaron

Cover art by L.J. at mayhemcovercreations.com

Editing by J. Brooks

ISBN: 0692529829
ISBN-13: 978-0692529829

OTHER BOOKS BY CELIA AARON

Magnate
The Acquisition Series, Book 2

Sovereign
The Acquisition Series, Book 3
***

The Forced Series
***

A Stepbrother for Christmas
The Hard and Dirty Holidays, Book 1

Bad Boy Valentine
The Hard and Dirty Holidays, Book 2

Bad Boy Valentine *Wedding*
The Hard and Dirty Holidays

F*ck of the Irish
The Hard and Dirty Holidays, Book 3
***

Zeus
Taken by Olympus, Book 1

Sign up for my newsletter at AaronErotica.com and be the first to learn about new releases (no spam, just send free stuff and book news.)

Twitter: @aaronerotica

CONTENTS

DEDICATION

To my readers: thanks for going lights out with me and
keeping our secret.

CHAPTER ONE
SINCLAIR

IN THE HEART of every man is a darkness. Primal. Instinctive.

At its most basic, it's a desirous nature—one that covets, demands, takes. Most men brick it up behind a wall of self-control. They invest time and effort in maintaining the separation. These men, good men, control the darkness until it withers away and becomes nothing more than a shadow haunting their innermost thoughts. Something easily forgotten, dismissed, erased.

I've never been a good man.

My darkness is neither restrained nor buried. It lives right at the surface. The only thing that hides it is my mask.

My mask is the law, the light, the pursuit of justice. It is forthright and airy. It is the appearance of righteousness in a fallen world.

The mask I wear is purely the act of a predator. Theater. Pageantry. Deceptive and lethal. It allows me to get close and closer still until it is time to strike.

I stalk so near that my prey can feel the tickle of my breath, the coldness of my heart, the depth of my depravity. Only a whisper separates me from what I desire.

Then the mask falls away, and all my victim sees is darkness.

CHAPTER TWO
STELLA

THE DISTRICT ATTORNEY sat completely still at the dark, polished table across the courtroom. My father sat in front of me at an identical table, but he was full of nervous energy. He shifted, ran a hand through his silver hair, and leaned over to whisper to his attorney.

I clasped my hands in my lap until the ring on my index finger dug into my flesh. This was the last chance my father had for freedom, the last day he would be able to throw himself on the mercy of the court. My gaze wandered back to the district attorney, the one who had my father arrested. Investigators scrutinized every last cent the old man ever invested or borrowed. And, just like that, my world became a smoldering heap of ashes. All because of one man.

Sinclair Vinemont was unmoving, like a spider poised on a web, waiting for the slightest sensation of movement from a hapless moth. My father was the moth, and Vinemont was about to destroy him. The investigation and prosecution had been the careful work of a master. Vinemont had woven the cocoon tighter and tighter until my father was caught from all sides. He had nowhere to run, nowhere to try and hide from Vinemont's poison. Dad was being systematically dismantled by the silent monster in a perfect suit.

I wanted to crumble. I couldn't. Dad needed me. No matter the long list of allegations and the even longer list of evidence against him, he was my father. He had always been there for me. Always protected me, stood by me, and encouraged me. Even after what my mother had done. Even after what I had done.

I would not leave his side. He was staring down a hefty prison sentence. Even if the worst happened, I would visit him, call him, write him, and keep him company until the day he got out. I owed him that and much more.

I stared at Vinemont so hard I hoped he would burst into flames from the sheer heat of my hatred. I'd wished for his demise for so long it had become like second nature to me. I hated him, hated every slick word from his mouth, every breath he took. Vinemont's downfall was stuck on replay in my mind. As I glared at his back, he remained tranquil, completely at ease despite my father coming apart with worry at the table next to him.

I forced myself to drop my gaze, lest anyone see me glaring at him with embittered rage. I couldn't bear for my father to suffer any further torment, especially not if it was based on any of my actions. My hands were pale in my lap, a white contrast to my dark pinstriped skirt. I took a deep breath and settled myself. It would do no good for me to fall apart now. Not in the face of my father's sentencing. I let out my breath slowly and looked up.

Something was different. I darted my gaze to the side. Sinclair Vinemont sat just as still, but now his eyes were trained on me. His gaze pierced me, as if he were seeing more than my exterior. I refused to turn away and, instead, gave him a matching stare full of righteous anger. We were locked in a battle, though not a word was said and no one threw a punch. I wouldn't look away. I wouldn't let him win even more than he already had. I perused his appearance more fully than I had ever dared. He would have been handsome—dark hair, blue eyes, and a strong jaw. He was tall, broad, fit. The perfect man except for the ice I knew coated his heart.

The internet had told me everything I needed to know about him. Single, old money, career in public service, and at twenty-nine years old, he was the youngest district attorney in parish history. The only thing I didn't know about him was why he would dare look at me, why he thought he had any right to pin me with his gaze after he'd ruined my life. I wanted to spit in his face, claw his eyes, and make him hurt the same way he'd hurt my father and me.

The door at the front of the courtroom opened and the judge entered, a stark, elderly man in black robes. Vinemont finally turned away, vanquished for the time being. Everyone in the courtroom stood. The judge shuffled to his seat behind a high wall of wood and state insignias, far above the spectators and lawyers.

"Be seated." Despite his apparent age, his voice boomed, echoing off the dusty shutters and up into the gallery above. "Counsellor Vinemont..." He trailed off, sorting through the papers on his desk.

My father sank into his chair and turned to grant me a thin smile. I tried to smile back to give him some sort of comfort, but it was too late. He'd already faced forward, watching the judge. I willed the judge to let my father go, to suspend his sentence, to do anything except take him away from me. I had no one else. No mother. No one except Dylan, and I refused to rely on him for anything.

Vinemont stood and fastened the top button of his suit coat before stepping from behind the table. He was tall, and like so many dangerous things, effortlessly beautiful.

The bespectacled, bearded judge was still rifling through sheets upon sheets of documents when Vinemont spoke.

"Judge Montagnet, I have several victims lined up to

speak against Mr. Rousseau." His deep Southern drawl was an affront to my ears. Even so, words spilled off his tongue with ease. He could charm the devil himself. As far as I was concerned, Sinclair Vinemont *was* the devil.

I wished we'd never left New York, never travelled to this backwoods bayou full of snakes. Vinemont condemned my father with airy ease every chance he got. No one spoke against him. No one countered his venomous lies other than the ham-handed defense attorney my father hired. So many of the people we'd met in this town were good, forthright souls—or so I'd thought. They weren't here. They didn't sit on my father's side to give him support against Vinemont's false charges. They hadn't come to testify that my father's sentence should be reduced or that he should be granted mercy. It was only me and rows upon rows of empty, cold pews. We were alone.

On Vinemont's side of the courtroom, two rows full of people, maybe twenty in all, sat and glared at Dad and me. Most of them were elderly men and women who had invested with my father. They blamed him for losing their money when all he did was invest as they requested. He had no control over the market, or the crashes, or the resulting instability. My father wasn't the monster Vinemont had made him out to be.

One of the women, gray and wrinkly, met my gaze and made the sign of the evil eye. I only knew what it was because she'd done it before, the last time I'd seen her in court during my father's trial. I'd looked it up and realized she was cursing me. With each movement of her hand, she was willing destruction down on my head. I looked away, back to the true reason for my father's disgrace and my desperation. Sinclair Vinemont.

The judge nodded. "Bring up your first witness, Counsellor."

I steeled myself as one by one, the alleged victims walked, limped, or wheeled past me to testify against my father. Their tears should have moved me, their tales of trust broken and fortunes lost should have forced some shred of empathy from my heart. All I felt was anger. Anger at them for getting my father into this mess. More than that, anger at Vinemont as he stood and patted the "victims" on the shoulder or the arm and gave out hugs like he was running for office. Every so often I could have sworn he leered back at me, some sort of smug satisfaction on his hard face.

The day droned on with story after story. With each witness, Dad slumped down farther in his chair, as if trying to melt away into the floor. I wanted to put my hand on his shoulder, tell him things could be fixed. Instead, I sat like a statue and listened.

The accusations stung me like a swarm of hornets. After the sixth or seventh witness, I went numb from their venom. Despite the breadth of the charges, I did not doubt my father. Not for a moment. Vinemont had done all this to ensure his reelection or for some other, similarly vile purpose.

When the last witness finally turned her walker around and shuffled back to her seat, the silence became a separate presence. Heavy, ominous, and draining, like a specter haunting the empty spaces of the room. My father remained hunched forward, his head bowed.

"Well, judge, I think you've heard enough." Vinemont held his hands out beside him, the show at an end.

"I have. I'm going to need the evening to think on the sentence." He glanced around the courtroom, his impassive gaze stopping on me for a moment longer than anyone else. "I'll have my verdict in the morning."

Vinemont turned to the judge and gave him a slight nod. Judge Montagnet returned the nod and then banged his gavel. "Court is adjourned."

"Just let me make you feel better." Dylan leaned over me, pushing me sideways onto the ancient leather sofa in my father's library.

"I can't do this right now." I tried to push him off but he pressed harder, overcoming my balance so I fell on my back beneath him.

He put his mouth to my neck, sucking my skin between his teeth. He was large and well-muscled thanks to endless lacrosse and rowing. He crushed me and constricted my chest.

"Please, Dylan." I gasped. I should have been afraid. I wasn't. I was still dazed from the courthouse. Dylan was just adding to the long line of disappointments I'd suffered over the past six months.

He pushed his knee between my legs.

"I can make it all go away for you," he murmured against me. "Just let me make you feel good for a minute. You need a break."

He forced his hand up my skirt.

"Stella? Where are you?" My father's voice calling my name had my stepbrother off me in a heartbeat.

Dylan gripped my hand and yanked me into a sitting position as he straightened his button-down and smoothed his blonde hair. He winked at me. The bastard.

When Dad didn't show up in the doorway, I knew it was the "come here" sort of call.

"I have to go."

"Later," Dylan whispered.

Not if I can help it. Dylan had taken one youthful mistake committed years ago and turned it into some sort of lifelong flame. No matter how many times I told him, he just didn't believe that twenty-five year-old me wasn't the same as the foolish, needy nineteen-year-old I once was.

When my father and I had moved to Louisiana, we were despondent. Mom had left this world without saying goodbye or giving an explanation. Dad and I were adrift, trying to come up with some way to carry on even though our heart was gone, buried in the cold ground of a New York cemetery.

Dad eventually took a liking to Dylan's mother and tried to make a new start with her and, admittedly, her family fortune. Neither venture worked out and they divorced after only six months. Dylan and I were mismatched step-siblings if ever there were any. I painted and read. He loved sports and abhorred learning of any sort if it didn't have to do with Xs and Os on a whiteboard.

Still, I was sad and desperately looking to feel something, anything, in the wake of my mother's death. Dylan was there and more than willing. So, I did something foolish. It was my first time—my only time—and I didn't exactly regret it afterward, I just didn't think about it. It was a non-event for me. That wasn't the case for Dylan, unfortunately.

I shook thoughts of him from my mind as I followed my father's voice to the back of the house and into his study.

Dad had sunk our last few dimes into this turn-of-the-century Victorian home. The whimsical façade was charming. The leaking ceilings and drafty windows? Not so much. Even so, it had been a safe place until Vinemont's tendrils had begun to invade, first with visits from investigators, then the arrest, then the searches. Vinemont had shown up each step of the way, reveling in the torment he inflicted.

For the millionth time that day, I hoped Vinemont would spontaneously combust. Then I strode into my dad's study.

The fire was crackling, and the room smelled of my

father's pipe. The atmosphere in that room always had a way of putting me at ease, making me feel safe. Even now, after all we'd been through, I still felt a familiar comfort when I walked in.

Along the back wall near the high windows, he'd arranged the draft paintings and sketches I hadn't sent to the local gallery. I'd caught him so many times just standing in front of whichever piece he'd decided to peruse for the moment, staring into it as if it held some sort of answer. My mother had taught me to paint. Maybe he was seeing her in the strokes and lines?

My feet hit the soft Persian rug that I used to play on as a child, bringing me back to the here and now. My father sat in his favorite wingback chair near the fire. The room felt fuller, somehow more occupied than usual, as if there was less air or not enough space.

Despite the crackling flames, the room was colder, darker. My familiar comfort drained away. Someone else was sitting in the matching chair facing my father, though I couldn't see who it was.

My pace slowed as I saw my father's stricken look. His wrinkled, yet still handsome face was pale, even in the flickering firelight. The first coils of dread snaked around my heart, constricting it slowly.

"Dad?"

Then I caught the scent of *him*. Whenever I passed him in the courthouse or when he came too close to where my father and I sat, I'd gotten a taste of this same scent. Woodsy and masculine with a hint of some sort of sophisticated tinge. My knees threatened to buckle but I kept going until I stood behind my father's chair and faced my enemy.

Vinemont's cold gaze appraised every inch of my body. "Stella."

I'd never heard him say my name. He spoke it with his signature arrogance, as if just uttering the word was somehow beneath him.

I scowled. "What is this? What are you doing here?"

"I was just discussing a business arrangement with your father. He doesn't seem inclined to accept my terms, so I thought I would run them past you. See if I got a different result."

"Get out," I hissed.

He smirked, though there was no joy in his eyes, just an inscrutable coldness that radiated out and made my skin tingle.

"I think you should leave." Dad's voice broke on the last word.

"Do you, now?" Vinemont never took his eyes from me. "Before I've had the chance to give Stella the particulars?"

I put my shaking hands on the back of my father's chair. "What are you talking about?"

"Nothing. Mr. Vinemont should be leaving." My father's voice grew a bit stronger.

"Y-you can't be here talking to my father without his attorney." I forced the tremor to leave my voice. "I know the law, Vinemont."

Vinemont shrugged, his impeccable dark gray suit rising and falling with the movement. "If you aren't interested in keeping your father out of prison, then I'll go."

He didn't move, simply watched me with the same dark intensity. Goosebumps rose along the back of my neck and shoulders.

What is this?

"What do you mean?" I asked. "How?"

"As I was just explaining to your father, I have a certain deal to offer. If you accept it, then he'll stay out of prison. If not, then he'll be going away for the maximum sentence—fifteen years."

"A plea deal? But you've refused this whole time to make any deal at all." My voice rose, anger influencing every word. "You were in the papers, telling anyone and

11

everyone that you would do nothing short of seeing my father rotting in prison."

"Plea deal? I never said anything about a plea deal. I didn't realize you were this foolish." He steepled his fingers and canted his head to the side. He looked like Satan, the firelight dancing along his strong features. "No, Stella. I already have a conviction, nothing left but sentencing for him. And I have no doubt he'll get the max. I've made sure of it."

He spoke as if I was a small, slow child in need of extra after-school help.

"Then what? What are you offering?" My hands fisted, my fingernails digging into my palms. "And what do you want in return?"

"Ding ding ding, she finally catches on." His smirk grew into a wicked grin that chilled every chamber of my heart. His teeth were even and white. If there had been actual warmth in the smile, he would have been beautiful. Instead, he was the monster from my nightmares.

"The deal is simple. Even simple enough for you to understand, Stella." He reached into his inner suit coat pocket and drew out a folded sheaf of papers with some sort of wax seal. "All you have to do is sign this and your father will never see the inside of a prison cell."

"No. I've heard enough. Get out of my house." My father stood and came around the chair to stand by my side.

Vinemont finally tore his gaze from me and glowered at my father. "Are you certain, Mr. Rousseau? You do realize that a Louisiana prison is hell on earth as it is, but I have ways to make it even more unbearable. Cell mates and such? It would be a shame for you to get paired with a violent—or amorous—sort, especially at your age. You wouldn't last long. Maybe a month or two until you broke. And after you're broken, well, let's just say the prison system isn't exactly known for spending medical dollars on old, decrepit thieves."

"Get out!" My father's voice rang out stronger than I'd ever heard it, even as he trembled next to me.

Vinemont's smile never faltered. "Fine. See you in court."

He tucked the papers back into his coat, rose, and strode from the room. Confidence permeated his movements as he stalked out like some big, dangerous animal. The sureness of his words, the conviction of his gait left me feeling at once chilled yet burning to know why he'd come.

What the hell is going on?

When he was gone, I was finally able to take a full breath. I clutched the back of the chair. "What was that?"

My father pulled me into his chest, his familiar smell of tobacco and books cutting through Vinemont's more seductive scent. He was quaking violently. "No. Nothing. Forget about it. About him."

"What did he want? What was in those papers?"

"I don't know. I don't care. If it has anything to do with you, I don't want it. I don't want him near you."

I leaned away and looked into my father's eyes. He didn't meet my gaze, only watched the fire behind me the same way he would stare into my paintings. He studied something far away, past the flames and the bricks and the mortar.

Fatigue was written in every line on his face. Not even the flickering orange glow could hide how drained, how frightened he truly was. He hadn't looked this haunted since the night he found me lying on the floor, almost two years ago. I rubbed my eyes, trying to erase his fear and the memories from my mind.

He let out a labored groan and fell back against the chair.

"Dylan!" I called.

My stepbrother appeared in the doorway within moments. "What's going on? Was that the dick prosecutor I passed in the hall?"

"It doesn't matter, just please help Dad to his room. He needs to rest."

"No, no. I'm fine." Dad clutched me to him again, his grasp weaker, fading. "I love you, Stella. Don't forget that. No matter what happens tomorrow."

I forced my heart to stay together. If it shattered, I would be of no use. I couldn't become a quivering heap of regret, not yet. Not until I found out what Sinclair Vinemont wanted from me.

CHAPTER THREE
SINCLAIR

I TAPPED MY fingers along the top of my thigh as I waited. I hated waiting. Something about it made me itch to do something, anything, to keep my life moving. Good or bad, it didn't matter. Given my history, most likely bad.

I wouldn't have to wait long. I knew she would come. The dutiful daughter, rushing after any salvation for her father she could find. Poor little idiot. Salvation had a price—the highest one imaginable—and I knew she would pay it the moment I first laid eyes on her.

She'd been sitting at her father's side at his arraignment. Her red hair had been pulled back in a tight bun and she wore a black suit, as if she were in mourning. She wasn't. Not yet. She would be soon enough. I'd caught sight of her as I walked through the door from Judge Montagnet's chambers.

It had been immediate—I wanted her. More than that, I wanted to break her, to make her mine and take everything from her until I was the only thing she thought, or dreamed, or breathed.

She seemed easily breakable. Her pale skin and delicate wrists with the tell-tale scars were like a lure to me, and her understated curves would look perfect when reddened by my hand or belt. But my momentary infatuation faded with each step closer I came to her downcast eyes. She'd be too easy, too quickly cowed and brought to heel. She wasn't a challenge, and I wouldn't waste my time.

But then she'd looked at me. Her eyes were fire, heat, hate. I wanted to stoke the flames, to make her despise me with even more ferocity. I knew how to get her there, to drag her down into the darkness and twist her beyond recognition. I would do it, too. There was no longer an 'if', only a 'when'. Things had been set in motion that were beyond even my control. She was my Acquisition.

I shifted in my seat and willed her to come to me. The sooner the ink dried on our deal, the sooner I could begin her education. The front door of the Rousseau estate opened, casting yellow rays of light onto the wide, curved stoop. Her small figure took the few steps down the stairs, and she strode toward my car with purpose. I couldn't see her face in the dark, but her movements were enough. She had steeled herself for this, strengthened every fiber of her being. I would tear it down piece by piece until she was naked, shivering, and begging for more.

My driver, Luke, got out and opened the back passenger door for her. She slid in next to me, though she took care to come no nearer than absolutely necessary. She still wore the light blue blouse and black skirt from earlier. The coat was gone, and she'd put on some unbecoming flats. I frowned.

"I should've known you'd be waiting out here like a spider."

I smiled at her. She would come to regret that statement. "What can I do for you, Stella?"

"What's this deal?"

I reached into my coat pocket and she jumped. She pressed herself back into the car door. Her fear made my cock spring to attention, annoying me. This wasn't about fucking her. This was about defiling her. Destroying her.

Adding her to a gruesome menagerie.

"As I said before, Stella, it's simple." I drew the document from my pocket and handed it to her.

She looked at it as if it were a particularly venomous snake before darting her hand out and taking it.

"Luke." At my command, my driver flipped on the interior lights.

Stella turned the documents over in her hand and stared at the large 'V' wax seal, covered in the classic vines that adorned the Vinemont crest and estate. "What is it?"

"A contract."

Her gaze shot up. She had dark half-moons under her eyes, and her skin seemed almost sallow in this light. She was worn down, or at least she thought she was. This was nothing compared to the coming months.

She studied my mask. Finding nothing there to enlighten her, she broke the seal and unfolded the contract. I'd written it myself in perfect calligraphy. She read through the recitals on the first page, which stated the parties to the contract, dates, duration, and other boring particulars.

"One year?" She said it to herself more than to me as she flipped to the second page.

Her eyes grew wider with each line she read, until a look of utter horror painted her face. It was beautiful. The paper shook as a tremor settled into her hands. She finished the page and flipped once more. The last page was simply for her signature.

It seemed impossible, but she shrank even further back, melding herself against the leather and metal of the car door. "You can't do this." Her eyes were glassy, fearful.

"I'm not doing anything. I've simply presented you with terms. You can agree to them or not. It's up to you."

"What will happen if I don't agree?"

"That's the question of a child, Stella. Worse, you already know the answer to it."

Her chin shook and her green eyes welled. "You'll send

my father to prison."

"No, I'll make sure your father *dies* in prison."

Her breath left her so quickly it was as if I'd punched her in the gut. And I had, in a way.

She recovered, though her voice was no more than a whisper. "But if I do agree—"

"Then you are mine for one year. To do with as I please when I please. You will live with me at the Vinemont estate. You will do as you're told. You will serve me and whoever else I want. I will own you, body and soul."

Though she trembled, she lifted her chin the slightest bit. "No one can own my soul."

I already do. "What's it going to be, Stella? This offer is quite time sensitive. Your father's sentencing is at eight a.m. sharp. And it's," I made a show of checking my watch, "ten fifteen p.m. right now. Tick tock."

"How do I even know you have the power to do this? How do I know you'll do what you say? I'm supposed to take the word of a man like you?"

A flame of anger licked around my heart. "Are you questioning my honor, Stella? I wouldn't do that if I were you."

She laughed, the sound shaded with exhaustion. "What is the word of a man like you worth? What sort of man presents someone with a slave contract and says 'sign it or your father dies in prison'? This isn't even enforceable. I may not be a *counsellor*, but even I know that."

She threw the pages back at me, adding more to her punishment. She was already poised to endure more pain in the next twelve months than she had for her entire sheltered life.

I neatly arranged the papers and pulled the final document from my coat pocket. This was sealed with a wax 'M'. I held it out to her. She ripped it from my hand and tore through the seal.

When her face fell, I was disappointed. No more fight?

No disbelief? No amazement at how completely I'd caught her in my trap? Instead, she just looked defeated. She *was* defeated, of course, but would it hurt her to lament her situation a bit more loudly?

"Judge Montagnet?" Her voice was barely audible now.

"Old family friend. You see, in this parish, old money has its own ways. This happens to be one of them. The North may have won the war, but slavery has always been in vogue around these parts. I don't choose based on color. That's barbaric. I choose based on certain other factors."

"Like what? Finding someone who will do anything to save the father she loves? Desperation? Is that it, you sick fuck?" The fire in her eyes was indulgent, alive.

Her punishments were adding up each time she opened her lips. Too bad I wouldn't taste them for a while yet. Not until she was broken beyond all repair and begged me to take her.

"Not quite. But that's all you need to know for now. What I need to know is whether you agree to my terms. As you see, Judge Montagnet has agreed to suspend your father's sentence for the year's time you agree to be mine. If at any time you breach this contract, Montagnet will immediately sentence your father and have him taken to the prison of my choosing. I rather like Dunwoody—no air conditioning and a widespread rodent infestation." I waited a beat, just to let the idea of rats crawling over her father while he slept sink into her mind. Then I continued, "So, as I've said from the start, it's up to you. The choice is yours."

I handed her back the contract. She took it, though I still wasn't sure if she'd rip it to pieces before my eyes. Her anger was unpredictable, wild. I wanted to taste it, take it in and relish it.

"Choice? You call this a choice?" She pushed her hair behind her ear in a violent movement.

"That's exactly what it is. Don't sign. Let your father

meet his fate. Or do sign, and give him a total reprieve." I relaxed back into my seat, though I kept my gaze on her.

She chewed her lower lip hard enough to draw blood. She didn't seem to notice. I wanted to run my thumb across her mouth and sample the flavor.

She stared past me, back into the warm light cascading through the front door of her house. "I can't decide on this right now. I need to get out of here. Away from you."

"I'm afraid that's not possible, Stella. I'm an early riser and, what with how late it already is, I'll need to be getting back home. So, you either stay here and I'll see you at the sentencing, or you come with me now and put the whole unpleasantness of the court system behind you and your father."

I smiled.

She cringed. Perfection.

I couldn't let her out of the car, not now that she was so close to signing. I could tell she was standing at the edge of the precipice, looking over the side and pondering the jump. Would the fall kill her? *Perhaps.*

She dropped her gaze to her lap. "How can you do this? You're supposed to uphold the law."

My hand itched to slap her for such a foolish question. For the pure naïve idiocy of it. But she wasn't mine yet.

"Public offices like mine are just a remnant of the *noblesse oblige.* It means nothing to me or my family. We couldn't care less if people like you rape and murder each other, or get hooked on drugs, or hurt their own kind. Enough questions. What's it going to be, Stella?"

"People like me?" Her eyes, shimmering with tears, found mine again.

My anger had reached its zenith. Her futile display of emotion wasn't going to change my plans. Nothing would. "For fuck's sake, Stella, sign it!"

She recoiled at my words and turned to open the car door.

Shit. I forced myself to remain still. I wanted to grab

her by the hair and drag her to me. I didn't. I let her finally find and pull the handle before she ran away and back into the house. The door slammed behind her, smothering the yellow light and leaving everything dark.

CHAPTER FOUR
STELLA

I DASHED PAST the library, narrowly avoiding Dylan as he came out into the hall.

"What—"

I ignored him and took the stairs two at time until I came to my room. I heard his heavy steps behind me but I slammed my door and clicked the lock over. I leaned back against the solid wood, my heart beating so loud that I thought my ears would burst from the pressure.

A hard knock at the door.

"Dylan, go away." It was more of a plea than a command.

"What's wrong?"

"I don't want to talk."

"Let me in." He twisted the handle, the metal parts clicking and scraping but not giving way.

"No. Just go. Please, Dylan."

"Who was that guy? Do I need to do something?"

Yes, you need to kill Sinclair Vinemont. "No. Just go."

The floorboards creaked, as if Dylan was walking in a circle outside my door.

"Dylan, please, just go back to your mom's house. I

need to rest. The sentencing tomorrow…"

The creaks stopped and a thump sounded, his hand hitting the door. "I'm sorry, Stella. About earlier. I just thought it would help is all. I didn't mean to cock things up even worse."

"You didn't. Really. I just, I just need to rest is all."

Another, lighter thump. "Okay. You're right. I'll go. See you in the morning. I'll be there for you."

I breathed a silent sigh of relief. "Thank you, Dylan."

His footsteps retreated and I sank down, my legs no longer willing to hold up the weight that grew heavier by the moment. I still clutched the contract to my chest. The infernal sheets of paper threatened to burn me down to nothing more than cold cinders.

I flipped the pages open and stared at the swirls and curves of ink. They had no meaning in the semi-darkness of my room. They were only drawings on a cave wall that told a story of violence and degradation. The elegant curlicues hid nothing from me. The words were stark, cruel—just like the man who'd written them.

I dropped the pages as if they scorched my fingers. The agreement fluttered to the floor and lay there as if it were just harmless paper. I knew better. I pulled my knees up and rested my head on them. How could I sign over my life to a man who I knew would hurt me? I had no doubt of it. The way he'd watched me in the car, as if I was a plaything, still haunted me. I'd been fearful of him before, of something I couldn't quite put my finger on. I still couldn't explain it, but now I was terrified.

Tears welled and leaked down my nose before landing on my knee and rolling down my leg. I sat like that for a long time. Minutes, hours. However long it took for me to go through my memories of my father. How strong he'd been when my mother had checked out of this life. How much stronger he had to be when I'd tried to do the same thing. Could I let him go to his death, all the while knowing I could have saved him?

One year. It wasn't so long. I'd wasted a year recovering from my suicide attempt. Would it be such a loss for me to disappear for one year? I'd never graduated college. My mother took her life the summer before I was to attend NYU. My life was put on hold indefinitely. Then Dad had decided to move us here so we could get on with our lives. Dylan's mother helped ease my father's pain for a time, though I withered away, locked in my room, painting dark scenes of even darker thoughts until it all became too much.

I shuddered at the memory of what I'd done. I'd vowed to never be weak again, to never let myself get to the point of wanting the oblivion badly enough to run headlong into it. I couldn't go to that place again. And just as I refused to rush to a dark fate, I refused to send my father to one equally grim.

I stood, my back stiff from resting against the unforgiving door. My decision made, I dragged a carry-on bag from my closet and began packing clothes, not caring whether they were fashionable. The basics would do— shirts, shorts, jeans, bras, socks, panties. I scooped up some toiletries from my bathroom and snagged the photo of my mother and me from my nightstand. I changed into a pair of jeans, a dark t-shirt, and a navy cardigan to protect against the chill in the fall air. After making quick work of my belongings, I pondered whether I should leave a note.

It tore at my heart not to say any goodbyes. I pulled out my stationery with the swirling 'S' along the top. I stood for a while with the pen poised over the page. My hand shook. There was so much to say. Or maybe there was nothing. The pen clattered from my fingertips.

I didn't trust myself. If I put what I felt down on paper, my resolve could waver. My father would know where I went, anyway. He wasn't a fool on any count. I only hoped he wouldn't do anything stupid to try and save me. He had no chance. The look on Vinemont's face when he'd proffered his bargain was one of certainty. If what I'd read about him was true—his family owning the largest sugar factories in America and some of the most expansive sugar cane plantations in a number of other countries—he had ways to keep my father at a distance. He and that snake Judge Montagnet would no doubt see to it.

I opened my bottom drawer and reached up for the knife I'd stashed there. I'd taped it to the bottom of the second drawer so that I was the only one who'd ever know where it was. It was the same blade I'd used on myself. My blood no longer stained the metal, but I knew parts of me were still there, ingrained in the steel. I shoved it into a side pocket of my bag, hiding it among some toiletries and underwear.

I gave one last glance around my room, saying a quiet goodbye, before creeping down the stairs and out to the garage.

I threw my few belongings into my trunk and started the car. It didn't take long to find Vinemont's address on my phone. It was an hour from town, out in the more rural area of the parish. Once satisfied I knew my way, I lay my phone on the small table next to the garage door. I couldn't risk anyone calling me and changing my mind. A plea from my father could break my resolve, and I was determined to see this through. For his sake.

I reversed down the driveway and settled in for the trip, watching the retreating façade of the house instead of the lane behind me. One year, and I would be back. One year, and my father would be safe.

What was one year to someone who should already be dead?

The drive was somber and dark. Though the moon was high, it was only a sliver in the vast expanse of inky black and scattered stars. The farther I drove from town, the more opaque my surroundings became. Night covered the fields of cotton, the groves of trees, and the brambles cloistering the dark waterways.

Soon the road withered down to two narrow lanes with woods encroaching on either side. I continued onward, though no cars passed anymore. It was just me, alone, being drawn ever forward into Vinemont's trap. I chewed at my lip, the taste of copper the only thing that stopped me from worrying away my flesh.

The road curved around to the left and the GPS told me the turn was up ahead on the right. All I saw were trees and thick underbrush, no sign of a house. I drove a little farther until I saw an opening. There was a drive of no more than a hundred feet that ended at a massive gate. I turned and idled up to it. It was wider than four cars sitting side by side and high. It was black wrought iron with metal vines twining and ensnaring the bars. In the center was a 'V', the vines slithering around the letter and creating an impenetrable barrier.

My breath caught in my chest. I looked around each side and saw the same high wrought iron fence flowing away from the gate and disappearing into the shadowy woods. I stopped and tried to calm my heart, to slow the hammering sensation of blood pounding through my veins.

Fear. There was no other word for it. The cold sweat along my temples, the sinking sensation pulling me down into despair. The deepest sort of dread overtook me, and I reached down to the gear shift, ready to put it in reverse and leave. Maybe there was some other way? Something I could do to save my father that didn't involve Vinemont, didn't involve whatever lurked beyond the sinister gate?

The metal shifted, swinging silently inward. There was no guard tower, no obvious camera anywhere along the unyielding metal fence. Still, he must have been watching me. I knew it just as sure as I knew I would be here, with him, for the next year.

I pulled my hand away from the shifter and rubbed a damp palm along my jeans. With a deep breath, I hit the gas and passed through the gate, lurching unsteadily forward into an unknown and uncertain future.

The driveway was initially hemmed in by the same forest and thick brush as the roadway. It was claustrophobic, even with the moon still high and clear in the sky. Slowly, the woods began to recede, leaving well-trimmed grass at the sides of the smooth drive. I'd gone what felt like a mile along the road, seeing nothing other than Louisiana landscape. Here and there would be a bridge crossing over dark waters as I flew past.

Ahead, the grass became expansive, a wide river of rippling emerald in the night breeze. Far in the distance, I finally saw lights glowing through the night. It must have been a house. *His* house.

I let off the accelerator, no longer fearing what dwelled in the dense woods and bayou inlets. Vinemont was a real, tangible danger, not one from my imagination.

Even as the grass expanded, more trees loomed ahead, forming an arch over the drive. These were the classic Southern oaks, moss hanging low from their limbs. Beyond the graceful trees was the home, a structure so tall that I couldn't see its roof for the blocking boughs. Three, possibly four stories of antebellum splendor—large columns anchored the palatial home, and it gleamed a ghostly white in the moonlight.

The windows were wide and tall, warm light spilling onto the porches. I could imagine rocking chairs and children playing tag, running through the grass, or having a picnic. But not here, not while Vinemont ruled over this estate. Despite the home's charm, its occupant lacked even basic human warmth. The magnificent façade was just that—charming camouflage for the depraved soul within.

I slowed and pulled up near the front door. The drive continued off to the right, further into the estate grounds. I took my keys from the ignition and was about to drop them into my purse. I stopped. Why? Would this car be sitting out here waiting for me for the year?

The thought made me laugh. My beat up American-made sedan sitting out in front of this mansion for a year, its battery going dead, parts rusting. It was absurd, just like everything that had happened over the past few months. I let the laughter pour from me. Some turn of the century medical pamphlet would say I had a case of 'hysteria' and advise that I be shipped off to the sanitarium. The giggles tapered off, as if I were sobering up. I didn't know if I'd have the chance to smile or laugh at anything again. Not for a year, at least, and something told me this year would leave scars to last a lifetime.

I dropped the keys in the cup holder and looped my purse over my shoulder before stepping out. I grabbed my bag from the trunk and rolled it to the steps. Mums, perfectly full of fall blooms, lined the flower beds next to the porch. I lifted my bag and rolled over the wide plank floor to the double front doors.

I didn't have to knock. A door swung inward to reveal an elderly butler. He looked stuffy and proper, though he had a smile for me. He was tall and wiry with white hair and light blue eyes. He seemed friendly, if reserved. The only odd thing was that he was getting the door for me at well past midnight.

"Miss." He gave me a small nod.

"Um, hi." I didn't expect this. I expected Vinemont to drag me in and beat me, hurt me, and throw me into a dungeon.

"Would you like to come in?" He smiled the slightest bit, as if amused by my hesitancy on the doorstep.

"I-I thought—"

"You thought what?" Vinemont stalked into the foyer. He wore a pair of dark jeans and a gray t-shirt. I'd never seen him in anything other than a perfectly-tailored suit. He seemed almost human. His chest was somehow broader than I remembered, tapering down to narrow hips and long legs. A five o'clock shadow covered the hard lines of his jaw and fluttered down his neck. His eyes were still cold, though, and as calculating as ever.

And there was something else about him I never thought possible—dark vines of ink snaked from under his sleeves and down to his forearms. He was like the wrought iron gate—cold, hard, and choked with equally unyielding greenery. His unexpected tattoos shocked me more than the surreal nature of my situation.

I closed my mouth, determined not to answer any of his questions.

"Do come in, Stella. We won't bite." He smiled.

I wanted to slap the look right off his face.

"Farns, this is our newest Acquisition."

The butler blanched and swayed. Vinemont put a hand on the old man's elbow to steady him. That one tiny act of kindness made me feel like I'd fallen into some alternate dimension. I didn't think 'kind' was something ever attributable to the spider standing before me.

Farns turned his head from Vinemont then back to me, his friendly smile faltering. "I see." He sighed. "This year? I see. May I?"

He held a shaking hand to take my luggage. I passed it to him.

"Thank you, Miss—?"

"It's Stella Rousseau," Vinemont said. "Go ahead and get the quilt room ready for her. I would have told you earlier, but I wasn't sure if she'd accept." The cold smile crept back into place as Vinemont continued assessing me.

I bristled. "I think you *were* sure. You knew all along, you bastard."

Farns coughed delicately. "Oh, well, I'll just go get everything straightened out for you, Miss Rousseau." Farns gave Vinemont a strange look, almost pitying, before taking my bag and heading toward the sweeping stairs.

I peered around, ignoring Vinemont. The house was just as beautiful inside as out. Antique wood and plaster work graced every surface I could see. The floors were a warm honey color, reflecting the light of chandeliers and sconces that bathed the rooms in warmth. The furniture was dark, providing a contrast and making everything look even more luxurious.

The room to the right had couches and an elegant writing desk. The one to the left appeared to be a music room. A piano, guitars, and a few other instruments were displayed. I realized the wall paper was actual sheet music, pieces pasted over other pieces until the room was a paper mache made of melody and harmony.

The Rousseau home back in town was large. This house would have swallowed it whole and come back for seconds.

"When you're finished gawking, we can get down to business." Vinemont was still sizing me up, maybe deciding how badly he intended to treat me. I didn't know. Everything was so foreign, so overwhelming. Even so, I forced my spine to straighten. I wouldn't let him intimidate me.

"Fine." I glared back at him.

He turned and walked past the staircase, leading me deeper into the house. The grandeur didn't end. Paintings and rich tapestries lined the halls. Some of the artists I recognized, others were a mystery, but I wanted to stop and inspect each one. Instead, I followed my captor. He drew me into a dining room with two bright crystal chandeliers overhead. The table sat at least two dozen people.

He went to a sideboard with a decanter and glasses atop it. "Have a seat. Want a drink?"

I was confused before. Now I was utterly lost. "A drink?"

He looked at me over his shoulder as he poured perfectly. "Yes, Stella. In everyday parlance it means a liquid refreshment. In this context, I'm suggesting an alcoholic beverage."

Asshole. "Yes."

"What's your poison?"

"Whatever you have."

"We'll have to work on your tastes."

I winced at the thought of Vinemont working on anything of mine.

I sank down into the nearest chair and lay my head on the back of my hands.

"What is this?" I mumbled. I wasn't sure if I was asking him or me.

"This is you and I having a drink as we discuss the contract. I assume you brought it?" He put a glass next to me, setting it down with a slight clunk.

He took the seat across from me.

I dug in my purse and pulled the pages out. "Yes."

"Good. Have you signed?" He took a drink from his glass, appearing nonchalant. He didn't fool me. There was eagerness in his eyes, the spider hungry for its next meal.

"No."

"But you're here, so I assume you intend to sign it?"

I leaned back and returned his direct stare. "Why won't you just let my father go?"

"Because he's a criminal."

"So are you."

He drained his drink. "No, I'm not."

"So slavery is legal all of a sudden? No one told me we'd revoked the Emancipation Proclamation."

The corner of his mouth twitched the slightest bit, as if his cruel smile wanted to surface. It didn't. "The real question, the one you keep avoiding, is whether you believe your father is a criminal." He stood and poured himself another drink before returning to the table.

I took my glass and turned it between my palms, the condensation wetting my fingers. Back and forth. "He's not."

"Then you really are as dumb as I think you are."

"That's fair, given I already know you're as evil as I think you are."

He smirked. "Evil? You haven't seen anything yet, Stella."

"Funny, I feel like I've already seen more than enough." I gave him a pointed look.

He pushed back from the table and walked around to my side before picking up the contract. His scent enveloped me. I could feel him, his eyes on me, as he stood at my back. He bent over and smoothed the paper with his large hand. I noticed a series of scars along the back of his wrist. They were faint, barely noticeable, but there all the same. A crisscross of damage marking his otherwise perfect hand. I had the wild instinct to run my fingertip along the scratches, to see if he really was made of flesh and blood. I didn't. I wouldn't.

"Just so happens I have a pen right here, Stella." He slapped down a fountain pen next to the signature page.

He leaned in closer, his mouth at my ear though he never touched me. "Sign it."

I closed my eyes, hoping I would open them and the nightmare would be over. It didn't work. The paper with my signature line was still in front of me, held in place by his strong hand.

I picked up the pen and poised it over the page. "Are you going to hurt me?" I hated the weakness in my voice, the weakness of the question, but I had to ask.

His warm breath tickled my ear. "Definitely."

My hand began to shake, my resolve faltering.

"But that doesn't mean you won't like it." He reached around me, his hard chest pressing into my back, as he steadied my hand with his own. "Sign it, Stella."

His voice was somehow hypnotic, seductive. Instead of loathing, something else bloomed inside me. It was sick, wrong. Even so, I leaned back into him the slightest bit, searching for some sort of comfort. He didn't withdraw.

His hand was warm, unlike his heart. He pressed down until pen met paper, the ink spreading like blood from a wound.

I should have tried to fight him, to burn the house down and run. But the wall of muscle at my back told me just how futile such thinking truly was. I would have to use other tools at my disposal if I wanted to make it through this ordeal.

I took a deep breath. *For Dad.* I moved my hand under his, making the swirling signature that bound me to Vinemont, that made me his, his to rule and ruin, for a year. When my signature was finished, the last letter inked, he leaned in even closer, the tips of his lips pressing against my earlobe, raising goosebumps down my neck and lower.

"Now you're mine, Stella."

With that, he seized the papers and stalked from the room.

CHAPTER FIVE
SINCLAIR

FUCK. THAT WAS not the way it was supposed to go. I paced around my study as Farns escorted Stella up to her room. What was I doing? It didn't help that my erection was siphoning blood away from my brain. No wonder I couldn't think straight.

I went to the closest half bath and locked myself in. I unzipped my pants, angry at the complication my dick was causing. It wasn't supposed to be like this. This transaction was solely business for me. Something that needed to be done. The same as it had been for other generations of Vinemonts. The same as it had been for centuries. I wasn't a special fucking snowflake. I was a Vinemont.

Of course, the last Acquisition had been done by my mother when I was still a small child, but I don't remember it going so badly straight out of the gate. She had followed the rules, respected the tradition. She was a true Vinemont, whereas I was standing in a water closet with my cock bossing me around. *Motherfucker.*

I pulled the traitorous length from my boxer briefs and began stroking. If I could just squeeze out a release, I would be able to calm down and do this the right way. I closed my eyes and saw her red hair, the way it fell around her shoulders as I'd stood behind her, the way it was begging to be fisted as I fucked her mouth. *No.* I forced my eyes open and looked at my own reflection.

I wouldn't think about her, not like that, not anymore. The time would come when I would fuck her, but not out of any real desire on my part, except for the desire to fully break her.

I fisted myself harder, pumping up and down as my hips bucked. An unwanted image of her guileless green eyes flitted across my mind. It was then my balls drew up tight and my cock jerked, shooting my seed into the delicate, hand-painted sink. Once I was done, I placed my hands on either side of the vanity and took a deep breath.

I had to maintain control. It was the only way to win. This year's Acquisition prize was mine for the taking. All I had to do was stay strong. I stared at myself in the mirror, willing the mask back into place. Once satisfied I was what I needed to be, I straightened.

I cleaned up, rinsed my seed down the drain, and tucked my cock back in. With this little momentary insanity behind me, I knew I would be able to maintain, to win, to ultimately defile Stella Rousseau.

CHAPTER SIX
STELLA

FARNS LED ME to an upstairs bedroom. He flicked on the light and showed me inside. The room was large and somehow light. I thought I'd be led to a cell with shackles and a metal bed. But no, this was a sweet country bedroom, even homier than my drafty room in town. It was along the side of the house, and two expansive windows filled one wall. Quilts hung along the other walls from floor to ceiling.

They were displayed with pride, some folded on racks and some spread out and exhibited. I scrutinized the nearest one with tired eyes. It bore a repeating pattern of a little boy in overalls and a wide straw hat. The fabrics were mixed, though all seemed well used.

"That one dates to 1897, I believe." Farns stood behind me.

"Does he collect these or something?"

"No, miss, he doesn't. His mother did, as did her father, and so on up the Vinemont tree."

"Who made them?"

"This one was done by a great-great grandmother of the late Mr. Vinemont. The rest were done by other

Vinemont women and sometimes men, if they had the knack of it."

There were so many others, some done in a similar style, others with art deco influences, some oddly modern. The room was a mix of old and new.

"This one," he pointed to a smaller square of material that was far darker than the others in the room, "was done by Mr. Sinclair's mother."

I ran my finger down a particularly straight seam. There was no pattern to the material, just jagged edges on blue and green fabric. The stitching was a deep crimson, discordant and striking.

"I didn't think people who have been rich forever bothered themselves with being useful."

"Forever is a long time, Miss Rousseau. Most things aren't quite so constant." He gave a slight bow and left, clicking the door shut behind him.

I needed more than veiled information, but I was too tired to follow Farns and ask questions. He wouldn't give me any real answers, anyway. Still, I went to the door and opened it. It hadn't been padlocked from the outside or anything. They had a strange way of keeping prisoners.

I pressed the door shut and eyed the bed. It was a four poster affair with a fluffy white comforter and welcoming pillows. I went to the closet and found it mostly empty. Farns had deposited my bag inside. Quilting fabric and thread were perched on the upper shelves, far from my reach.

I pulled out some toiletries from my bag and took them to the en suite bathroom. It was large for such an old house. Soaking tub, small walk-in shower, vanity, and toilet. I arranged my items in the cabinet and along the sink before getting ready for bed. It was odd, doing these things in a strange house, but I did them anyway. Brushing my teeth and changing into a t-shirt somehow put a veil of normalcy on the whole sinister affair.

I returned to my bag and dug out the knife. Tape still

lingered on the blade. I pulled out the third drawer of the bedside table and affixed the knife to the bottom of the second drawer, just like at home. No one would find it there. It was like an insurance policy of sorts. I didn't intend for it to ever spill my blood again. But Vinemont's? That was a definite possibility.

Once satisfied it was hidden, I sat down on the bed. It was plush, luxurious. I was through the looking glass—nothing made sense and everything seemed somehow backwards. Was it a trick? Would Vinemont drag me from my bed after I'd fallen asleep and throw me into a musty dungeon?

I rubbed my eyes, too confused and exhausted to ponder what would happen in the next few minutes, much less in the hours to follow.

I got up and hit the lights. The darkness was almost a comfort to me, like it was cloaking me from prying eyes. I crawled into the unfamiliar bed, sliding between the smooth sheets. They smelled like linen and faintly of detergent. Clean and cool against my skin. These things, this room, they were all meant to seduce me, just like Vinemont's voice in my ear. I wasn't in a fairy tale. Vinemont wasn't my prince.

I snuggled in deeper, hugging an extra pillow against me. It was down-filled, soft and fluffy. I breathed in deeply and let it out. I would enjoy what I could while I could, because I didn't know what tomorrow would bring. Sleep fell like a curtain in front of the stage, slowly obscuring me from view.

A knock at the door jarred me awake. Light streamed in through the windows, giving my cell the appearance of a traditional Southern room.

"Who-who is it?"

"Farns, miss."

"Oh, come in." I sat up and pulled my blanket to my neck.

He opened the door and took only a single step inside. "Breakfast is ready downstairs. I wanted to let you sleep for a while longer, but Mr. Sinclair has requested your presence."

"I haven't even showered." I pushed my hair back from my eyes, knowing it was a tangled mess.

"Even so." He didn't look at me. In fact, he looked everywhere but in my direction. Modest much?

"Fine. I'll be down in a few minutes." I paused, realizing I had no idea which way to go to get down to breakfast.

"I'll wait while you ready yourself and then I'll escort you, if you'd like," Farns said.

"Yes, please." I dropped the blanket and swung my legs over the side of the bed.

Farns backed out of the room and eased the door shut with a soft click.

I rose and stretched before going to the bathroom, washing my face, and running a brush through my hair. Presentable. But why should I be? Maybe when Farns said "breakfast" he really meant "guillotine" or "the rack." I had no way of knowing at this point. Were his kindly words and face just another put-on like Vinemont's?

I donned another pair of jeans, a tank top, and a cardigan. I wasn't sure about shoes, so I put on some sneakers. I sat for a moment to collect myself, to try and sort through what was true and what was the lie. It was impossible. I only knew one thing for certain—Vinemont was my enemy. Anyone connected with him was suspect, if not an outright danger to me. With that cold thought, I took a deep breath, straightened my back, and went to the door.

Farns was, as he promised, waiting outside. "Right this

way, miss."

I followed him down the long hallway. I peered into rooms as I passed. They were all bedrooms in this part of the house, each with a different theme. Some were flowery, others done in rich, dark fabrics.

"So, do you treat all your prisoners like this?" It came off even more snide that I'd meant it to. I was testy, angry, a seething bubble of emotions that seemed to have simmered overnight while I slept and only now erupted at my surface.

Farns stopped and then took another step, as if unsure whether to continue. "I'm not entirely sure how to answer that."

"Why? I'm sure I'm not the first slave Vinemont has owned."

"I, ah. Well, miss, you are the first Acquisition we've had for the past twenty years, if that's what you mean."

"Acquisition? I keep hearing that word. What does it even mean? Is it some code so you don't have to say 'slave'?"

He turned toward me, his eyes kind. He made it hard for me to be cross with him. "I take it Mr. Sinclair hasn't explained the Acquisition trials to you yet?"

"There are *trials?*"

"Yes, there are." Vinemont strode down the hall toward us. "And if you would come downstairs to breakfast, I would explain them to you."

I crossed my arms over my chest. "What's the rush?"

"Farns." Vinemont's gaze darkened and he waved the butler away.

Farns hesitated and then obeyed, retreating back the way we'd come until it was just Vinemont and me. He wore another pair of dark jeans with a black t-shirt, his inked vines snaking down his arms from beneath the fabric. In the morning light, I saw they were a deep green, small leaves done in an emerald, and vicious thorns done in almost black.

He gripped my upper arm and yanked me to walk alongside him.

"Hey—"

"You are testing my patience, Stella." He stopped and pushed me up against the wall. His eyes bored into me. "Don't ask Farns questions like that. He can't help you."

"I can ask whatever the hell I want." The cocktail of emotions roiling inside me had made me bold, even in the face of Vinemont's wrath.

His gaze travelled over my face, down to my lips and then back to my eyes. "That's where you're wrong."

He gripped my hair and pulled my head to the side. His mouth was at my ear again, his Southern drawl whispering darkly to me. "I thought I made it clear that I own you now. You do as I say. If you don't, I'll make sure your father feels the brunt of your punishment."

He stepped into me, pressing my back into the wall and crushing me painfully. I yelped at the sudden aggression. He clapped his free hand over my mouth. I hit ineffectually at his sides, his back. I even tried to knee him, but he took advantage of my efforts and pushed one of his large thighs between my legs and lifted so I was straddling him.

"Fuck." It was a gravelly whisper.

My heart beat faster and faster, panic welling up inside and drowning out any other emotion. He was going to hurt me. Right here, right now in this sunny hallway.

He pulled my hair harder and harder until I thought he would rip it out. I stopped struggling.

"Better. Here's how this is going to go, Stella. You are going to stop trying to make trouble. You are going to do as you're told. This year will pass by much easier for you if you just follow my orders. You can fight me." His lips moved down to my neck, a hairsbreadth from making contact. "And I'm not going to lie, I like it when you fight. It makes this easier for me. But you won't like the results."

He released me and backed away. He ran a hand

through his hair as he continued to stare me down. My heart hammered, demanding that I run as far and as fast as I could.

He licked his lips, reminding me of a hungry killer that had scented blood. *My* blood. I shivered under his gaze, hating that my nipples had hardened from the sensation of him rubbing against me.

Vinemont stabbed a finger in the air in the direction he'd come. "Go."

I bolted from the wall and tore down the hallway. I found the stairs to my right and maneuvered down them so quickly I almost fell on the second landing. His steps sounded behind me, heavy and deliberate.

I whirled when I reached the bottom, my stomach growling from the smell of food on the air. I turned right, spotting the front door. I didn't make a choice. My body made it for me.

I ran to the door and wrenched it open. I took off across the porch and down the stairs. The morning sun made the wide expanse of grass seem manageable. The air was crisp, fall had finally settled even this far south.

My sneakers barely touched the pavement of the driveway before I was treading on the soft earth. I ran as hard as I could. I was small. I would make it to the trees and hide. Just curl up somewhere in the roots of a cypress or maybe even climb and hide in the branches. Maybe Vinemont was lying about having the judge in his pocket. Maybe I could go to the police or someone else. I was desperate to believe it as I hurtled through the sunlit lawn.

None of my hopes were true, I knew that, but I didn't care as long as my legs kept pumping, carrying me closer to the salvation of the tree line. I had to get away from him, from the terror, from the flare of unwanted heat he sparked in me.

My lungs began burning, making me painfully aware of my need to stop and take deep gulps of air. I didn't. I pushed myself harder, ignoring the pain in my side, ignoring everything except the approaching sanctuary. I'd made it more than halfway across the emerald field.

I fell. Hard. Arms had encircled my waist and dragged me down so I was lying on my stomach. The grass had softened the fall, but not much. The air whooshed from my already tortured lungs, and my ribs felt on the verge of cracking apart and spearing the organs inside. The smell of fertile earth and verdant green invaded my nose, but his scent mixed in as well.

He was on my back. He gripped my arm and pulled me over roughly. He straddled me, his thighs against my hips. I couldn't see his face. The sun was high behind his head, blinding me. I screamed and tried to slap him, scratch him, draw any sort of blood I could. He captured my wrists easily and pinned them over my head. He leaned over me, blocking the sun yet showing me the scorching anger in his eyes. He was fierce, far worse than he had been upstairs.

"I warned you, Stella. I told you." His breaths were shuddering even as I gasped for air.

He transferred both my wrists to one of his hands and drew back his palm to strike me. I held his gaze. I wanted him to feel it, to know how much I loathed him, to know what I thought of his twisted soul.

His eyes opened a little wider at my stark stare.

"Fuck!" He stayed his hand and, instead, slammed his fist into the ground next to my head. He let out a roar, guttural and full of pent up rage.

He let my hands go and sat back, crushing my thighs. His head was thrown back, as if he were pondering the shape of the lazy white clouds above instead of thinking about how to hurt me. I lay still, once again blinded by the sun.

"You're killing your father." He brought his head back down slowly. His face was calm again, as if some switch had flipped.

"N-no." My breaths were finally evening out, though my head pounded from the adrenaline and lack of food.

"Yes, you are." He leaned down over me, bringing his face only an inch from mine. His erection was hard against my thigh. "If you had escaped, what do you think I would have done? Nothing?"

"I-I didn't think—"

"Exactly. That's your problem." He drew a hand up and fastened his palm around my throat.

I tried to pry his fingers off, scratching him and pulling. He didn't move, only squeezed harder the more I fought. It was as if he were pinching my windpipe, stopping even the slightest flow of air. When the edges of my vision started to dim, I relaxed.

"I thought I made it clear upstairs. I guess I didn't. What do I have to do to get through to you? Hurt you more? Take more?" He ran his free hand down my side, my stomach, and finally to the vee of my thighs.

I whimpered as he rubbed against the seam of my jeans, right over my clit.

"I will, if that's what you want, if that's what it takes for you to understand how completely I own you." He rubbed harder, building a heat inside me. My stomach clenched. I didn't want his pleasure, not like this, but my body wasn't discriminating.

"Is that it, Stella?" He eased his mouth closer to mine as his fingers continued to work. He was so close I could feel his warm, minty breath on my lips. "I've wanted you from the moment I saw you. Before I even planned on making you my Acquisition. What do you taste like? I wonder. I've wondered it for quite some time. Would you like me to find out?"

His fingers continued their maddening pace, forcing desire to swell where there should have been none, where there should be terror and anger instead. I couldn't stop the breathy sound that erupted from my lips.

He laughed, low and husky. "You would like for me to taste you, wouldn't you?"

My hips rose toward his hand of their own accord,

wanting more from him. He froze and blinked, as if realizing what he was doing.

"Shit!" He rose up and fell back as if I'd burned him. He sat in the grass at my feet, looking at me like I was a live grenade.

I sat up, blood rushing to my cheeks at how I'd reacted to his unwelcome touch. I saw movement behind him. I shielded my eyes from the glare of the sun and saw a young man, late teens or early twenties, walking up. He had sandy blonde hair, much lighter than Vinemont's, and his features, though similar, were softer, friendlier. He waved.

I dazedly returned it, not knowing what to do. Vinemont turned and saw the newcomer.

"Teddy, go back inside." It was a command, but lacking Vinemont's usual viciousness.

"What's going on, Sin?" The young man kept on his path until he stood at Vinemont's back. "Who's she?"

"She's none of your concern." Vinemont stood and faced him. "Go on in. We'll be in for breakfast in two minutes."

Teddy looked from me and back to Vinemont. "You sure?"

"Yes, I'm sure. It's nothing. Trust me."

Teddy's gaze landed on me, no doubt taking in my disheveled appearance. "Okay, Sin, if you say so. It's nice to meet you, um…"

"Stella. Her name is Stella Rousseau."

"I guess I'll see you at breakfast, Stella." Teddy wrinkled his brow, but eventually took Vinemont at his word. I was glad to see I wasn't the only one who made the same mistake.

Vinemont ruffled the boy's hair as he turned to trudge back to the house.

Are you shitting me? A hair ruffle from Vinemont?

"Up, Stella. Now." A growl for me.

I could either keep fighting and running or acquiesce.

Vinemont had already threatened my father again. I believed him. He was serious, lethal. The thought of my father in prison grounded me, reminded me of what I had to do.

I had no choice. I'd signed it away. Running had been instinctive. Now, I needed to calculate, to somehow figure a way out of this mess and keep my father and myself alive.

Vinemont offered his hand with an irritated sigh.

CHAPTER SEVEN
STELLA

FARNS GREETED US at the door. He didn't say a word as we walked by, but he gave me a kindly smile. I followed Vinemont past the now familiar stairs and into the main hallway that led deeper into the house. We passed the dining room from the night before and kept going, the smell of bacon and biscuits increasing the farther we went.

"Try and behave yourself for once," he grated, and turned left into a sunny breakfast room. The table here was smaller than the dining room's, able to seat only twelve. Teddy, the young man from the yard, sat toward the far end and chatted with a pretty maid. When we walked in she stiffened and scurried away.

"You know that's not allowed, Ted."

"What? Talking to the staff is a bad thing?" He grinned.

"Talking, no. Anything else, yes. You're a Vinemont. You can't lower yourself."

Teddy rolled his eyes. "C'mon Sin, I was just getting to know her a little. No big deal." He forked a piece of pancake and stuffed it in his mouth unceremoniously. He pointed the tines at me and mumbled something around his food that could have been "who's this?"

"I told you. Stella Rousseau." Vinemont motioned for me to sit across from Teddy while he took the seat at the head of the table.

The young maid from earlier brought in two plates already piled high with grits, pancakes, bacon, and scrambled eggs.

"If you'd like more of anything, or something different, please let me know." She curtsied and smiled, showing a youthful beauty. "Would you like coffee, tea, juice, or water?"

"I'd love some coffee." My system needed a jolt of caffeine to recover from the run.

"Yes, ma'am." She left and promptly returned with a coffee decanter and cups for both Vinemont and me. She asked my preferences on cream and sugar, but didn't ask Vinemont. She already seemed to know his desires. Once done, she gave Teddy a small smile and returned through the door behind him, to what I supposed was the kitchen. Teddy winked at me. He was a flirt, for certain.

"Okay, now we're alone. Tell me what's going on. You've never brought a woman to breakfast. Honestly, I don't think you've ever brought a woman to the house." Teddy stuffed another piece of pancake in his mouth and smiled.

"If you must know, she's my Acquisition." Vinemont took a long swig of the coffee, even though it was still far too hot.

Teddy sputtered around his pancake before swallowing hard and almost choking. His face reddened, his eyes watering. "That's us? It's us this year?"

I listened intently as I sampled the array the maid had provided. The food was delicious and much needed. I felt like I hadn't eaten in days. The information flying back and forth was even more satisfying.

"It is." Vinemont ripped off a piece of bacon and chewed slowly.

"What is it, really? I know sort of what it is, but not the whole thing." Teddy looked at me, all his prior flirtation gone.

"I'm not going to discuss this right now. I'm the eldest brother so it falls to me to take care of it. You don't have to worry about it. Needless to say, I want you to treat her with respect, and also to respect my decisions as they pertain to her. Understand, Teddy?"

He put his fork down. "What does that mean?"

"That means you may disagree or even hate some of the things you see or hear, but she is my responsibility and these things must be done."

"Why?"

Vinemont pinched the bridge of his nose. "Because they must."

"Okay, but *why*?"

"Goddammit, Teddy!" Vinemont slammed his fist down on the table.

Teddy jumped and seemed genuinely uneasy. Had he never seen his brother act like this? I could give him a lesson or two about the real Vinemont.

Vinemont placed both palms flat on the table and took a deep breath. He seemed as if he were trying to hold himself together somehow. "Let me give you an idea of what I mean." He turned to face me. "Stella, take off your clothes and stand on the table."

I stopped mid-chew. "What?"

"You heard me."

I looked at Teddy. His eyes were wide, the blood fading from his face as it did the same from mine.

"Don't look at him, Stella. You're not his. You're mine. You will do as you're told or you will be punished. Strip. Unless you'd like me to call Judge Montagnet?"

His threat spurred me into action. I stood.

Teddy did, too. "No, Sin."

"Teddy, sit down. You need to learn how things are done. I've coddled you for far too long."

Teddy backed away from the table as I lifted the hem of my shirt, pulling it over my head with shaking hands. Tears burned behind my eyes, at the back of my throat, but I did what he said. I couldn't risk not obeying.

"No, Sin, make her stop!" Panic filled Teddy's plea.

"Sit. Down." Vinemont's jaw was tight.

Teddy obeyed. Just like I did. Just like everyone under this roof must.

I unbuttoned my pants and drew down the zipper before shimmying out of them. I took a deep breath, hatred burning in my breast for Vinemont, even though he wasn't looking at me. He was focused on Teddy, where the real battle for control was being waged.

Now only wearing my bra and panties, I put a foot on the nearest chair to climb onto the table.

"I said all of it, Stella, or did you not hear me?" Vinemont's cold voice was quiet.

Bastard. A sob tried to escape, but I wouldn't let it. I reached behind my back and unclasped my bra, a single tear sliding down my face. My mind was screaming, roaring, crying. On the outside, I was placid. Only the uneven fall of tears gave me away.

I pulled my bra off and dropped it in the chair where I'd been sitting moments before. Teddy darted his gaze away. With shaking fingers, I pulled my panties down and kicked them aside.

"Look at her, Teddy." Vinemont fixated on Teddy. "Look!"

Teddy turned his face to mine, his kind eyes now fearful.

"Up on the table. Stand there."

I pulled a chair back and stepped into it before climbing up onto the table. The polished wood was slick and cold beneath my bare feet.

"Face me, Stella." He still stared down Teddy, forcing the boy to watch my every move.

More tears escaped, landing on my breasts and rolling

down to my stomach. I dropped my head, fixating on the table beneath me. Humiliation flowed through me like blood, or maybe more like gasoline, fueling my hatred yet explosive at the same time.

"Do you understand now, Teddy? Is it clear?"

"Y-yes."

"Good. Now finish your breakfast." Vinemont took another long swig from his coffee and attacked his food.

Teddy picked at what remained on his plate. "Are you just going to make her stand there?"

"I can make her do more, if you'd like."

Teddy slammed down his fork. "That's not what I meant and you know it."

"This is necessary. It's what has to be done. Get used to it." That was the Vinemont I knew, cold and unforgiving. Maybe he was right. Maybe the sooner Teddy realized his brother was a monster, the better.

Vinemont still hadn't looked at me. Coward.

A whistle sounded at my back. Vinemont's head whipped up, but he didn't look past me. Instead, he focused on me, taking me in, taking everything from me. His expression turned from anger to something else. He stood and froze, tension rolling off him in waves.

"Lucius, glad you could join us." Vinemont's gaze travelled my body. His stare was possessive, desirous.

I wanted to cross my legs, cover myself somehow. I knew he wouldn't allow it. So I stood, letting the degradation wash over me.

"So this is the Acquisition?" A man, his voice similar in tone to Vinemont's, yet silkier.

"Yes." Vinemont's gaze was still on me, as if he didn't want to give me up.

I maintained eye contact, damning him for doing this to me. I hoped he felt every flame of my rage. I hoped it charred his already black heart to ash.

A hand running up the back of my leg startled me and I jumped away. My foot tripped over the edge of the table. I hurtled down.

Someone caught me and set me on my feet. Vinemont pressed me into him, my face lying against his hard chest. For once, I was happy to be near him, happy to be at least somewhat covered. His hands were warm on my skin, his palms damp. Had he been sweating my forced exhibition?

"She's skittish, huh?"

I whipped my head around. Lucius was tall, lanky, and had similar tattoos as Vinemont. He wore a blue plaid shirt, the buttons at the top casually undone and the sleeves rolled up. His hair was a tousled brown, slightly lighter than Vinemont's and darker than Teddy's. Another brother?

"She's mine, Lucius. I was just teaching our little brother that lesson." Vinemont's voice rumbled against my ear.

Lucius arched an eyebrow before snagging a piece of bacon from my plate and devouring it. "I think all you taught Teddy was that a wanking is absolutely necessary ASAP."

Teddy stood. "I can't take any more of this mindfuck. I'm going into town for the day."

He fled the room in a huff. I envied him.

Lucius kept his gaze on my ass, the one piece of me that wasn't pressed against Vinemont. "She's definitely a prize. Think you'll get to be Sovereign? I'm still not clear on all the rules, by the way."

"Only the firstborn knows the rules. You're just guessing," Vinemont growled.

The tension in the room took on another dimension, thickening the air like invisible smoke.

"Then tell me already." Lucius pointedly licked the bacon grease from his index finger as he continued staring at my exposed rear.

Vinemont released his hold and pushed me behind him. I was beginning to agree with Teddy about the mindfuck. First he wanted to exhibit me and now he wanted to hide me?

"That would be breaking the rules. You aren't a firstborn."

I peeked around Vinemont.

"Fine." Lucius shrugged. "I'll just enjoy the show. I know enough from what Mother told us. This should get entertaining pretty fast. When's the ball?"

"Friday."

"You mean tomorrow? Damn. You waited pretty late to collar your Acquisition." He sprawled in the chair next to mine. "Laura!"

The pretty maid hurried in but stopped as soon as she saw me. Vinemont put a hand on my hip, possessive. She recovered far more quickly than I would have in this situation and poured Lucius a cup of coffee before fetching a plate of food for him.

"Thanks, babe." Lucius grinned at her.

She retreated, but not before casting another worried glance in my direction.

"I trust you'll stay out of my way as far as the Acquisition is concerned?" Vinemont's fingertips dug into me.

"Yeah, what do I care? It would be nice if you'd share, though you've never been particularly good at that."

The pressure increased, his whole hand palming my hip. "Just stay out of my way."

Lucius waved his fork in the air. "Fine. Carry on with your sadism. Ignore the man behind the breakfast plate."

"Get your clothes." Vinemont removed his hand, the warmth gone and leaving goosebumps in its wake.

I crept from behind Vinemont. Lucius watched every move intently as he chewed. I darted around behind him and snagged my jeans, shirt, bra, socks, and shoes, but I couldn't find my underwear.

I pulled the shirt on over my head and hastily yanked on my jeans. Once covered, I peered around the base of the chairs looking for any sign of my wayward panties.

They weren't where I'd left them, and I couldn't find them on the floor.

"Lucius, give them up," Vinemont said.

"Give what up?" He shrugged and turned to me. His eyes were lighter than his brother's, sky blue instead of the dark depths of Vinemont's. Lucius gave me lascivious wink.

I didn't think it was possible to like someone less than I liked Vinemont. I may have been wrong.

Vinemont stabbed his fingers through his hair and let out a particularly vile curse before turning toward the door. "Come on, Stella."

I followed Vinemont, but before I left the room, I turned. "I haven't had a shower yet today. Just so you know."

Lucius smiled. "Mmm, I like it best when they've soaked a bit."

Motherfucker.

"You're only encouraging him." Vinemont pulled me down the hall.

"Get your hands off me." I yanked my arm away from him.

"Fine," he snarled. "Just go the fuck upstairs. I can't deal with this right now."

"*You* can't deal with this? Are you kidding me?"

"Stella, I'm warning you." He advanced, crowding me back into the wall.

"I'm not afraid of you." I tried to put the force of my conviction into my words. It was a lie. I was scared, confused, and more alone than I'd ever been.

His hand was at my throat in an instant. "You and I both know that's not true. Get the fuck upstairs. Stay there until I come for you." He squeezed for emphasis before letting me go.

I slipped away from him, stumbling over the edge of the hall runner before righting myself and hurrying away. I looked over my shoulder. He stood perfectly still and watched me. I got the strange feeling that I was one wrong move away from him pouncing on me.

He was a predator by nature.

Right then I knew. If he acted on instinct, he would rip me to shreds.

CHAPTER EIGHT
SINCLAIR

THE MEMORY OF her naked body was forever seared into my mind. I was weak, so fucking weak. I'd thought forcing her to stand on the table was a show of strength, some way to teach Teddy the realities of our lives. Instead, I'd made myself almost blind with lust and gave Lucius a reason to torment Stella. She was *mine* to torment, no one else's.

I wanted to destroy every fucking thing in the house, then rage through the grounds like a tornado before lighting the woods on fire. Instead, I stepped out the front door and into the cool air. I needed a ride. Something to clear my mind and get me focused on the Acquisition trials.

I walked the few hundred yards to the shop out back. It was two stories of distraction. Fast cars, even faster bikes, and all the tools needed to repair each one of them. I ran my fingers down the McLaren, thinking it might be the one to take me far away from here—and as quickly as I needed. But the air was too nice to miss.

I snagged my leather jacket from the wall and chose Emelia instead. She was a revved up American stunner, a motorcycle my father and I had brought back to life years ago. I threw a leg over and cranked her up. She rumbled and purred beneath me. I tore from the shop, taking the road deeper into the Vinemont property.

The helicopter waited on the pad to my left as I cruised by. It wasn't an option. I had to keep my feet on the ground. It would be a simple feat to climb into the cockpit and simply fly away from this house, my responsibilities, and my Acquisition. I wouldn't. I needed to stay, to shepherd Stella through the trials.

Despite the setbacks, breaking her would be a singular treat. What I'd shown Teddy had only been a taste, just the tip of the proverbial iceberg. She had no idea what was in store. I wasn't even sure how far I'd go, but I knew I had to win. Losing wasn't an option.

I gunned the engine harder, rushing past the lake, the scattered cattails bleeding into a brown and green blur as I drove to the levee.

But the way she'd looked, the way she'd reacted to me in the grass, her smell, the way she fought. *Fuck.* I was screwed. I had to stop thinking about her as a *her*. She was an Acquisition—my Acquisition—and nothing more. If I didn't get my head on straight, and get her outbursts under control, tomorrow night would be a disaster. The Sovereign needed to leave the party knowing that my Acquisition was the one to beat, literally and figuratively.

I'd never actually attended an Acquisition Ball, but Mother had told me plenty in her attempts to strengthen me. The depravity in her tales had shocked me, intimidated me. She didn't go easy, telling me exactly what I'd have to do to win. In the process, she'd told me what she'd had to do to win during her Acquisition year. How a piece of her had died. She'd wanted me to endure, to make it through unscathed. To be even stronger than she had been.

I slowed to a stop in the middle of the levee, water sparkling on either side. My thoughts strayed back to the scars on Stella's wrists and the knife she'd hidden in her nightstand. I'd almost taken it from her as she slept. My fingers had traced the handle, the blade. Somehow I knew it was the same one she'd used on herself. Ultimately I'd left it there. I shouldn't have. Another mistake.

The engine roared to life beneath me and the bike ate up the smooth road through the woods and over the waterways. Wild turkeys scattered as I raced through their territory. I made the entire loop around the property before cruising down the winding lane and out to the front gate.

Approaching the bottleneck of woods and metal, I saw the glint of something metallic through the bars. A car sat on the outside, foolishly seeking entrance to my territory. I grimaced at the idiocy of the attempt, the sheer lack of understanding this visit revealed. Still, I knew he'd come.

I pulled to the right so I could stand broadside against the wrought iron. When I killed the engine, a heavy silence fell.

"Mr. Rousseau. Nice to see you."

He peered through the bars and vines, his eyes red and watery. There was nothing to see. Only me.

"Let her go." His wavering voice made me sick.

"No."

"You, motherfucker!" A younger man leapt from the car and rushed over. "Bring her out or we're coming in."

I laughed. "That's adorable. If there's nothing else, I'd best be going. Pressing matters and all."

He gripped the bars and tried to shake them. Nothing. This fence could withstand a lot more than some prep school prick in lacrosse gear.

"Dylan, stop. We can't win that way."

"Listen to the old man, Dylan." I let the venom that had welled up inside me over the past twenty-four hours infect my words.

"Please." It was a teary plea from Mr. Rousseau. "Just let her go. I-I'll go to prison willingly if you'll just let her go."

Pathetic. "Too late. The deal's done. If that's all the business you have to transact, I'm sorry to say you wasted your trip. Goodbye, Mr. Rousseau."

Dylan erupted in yells and a respectable amount of profanity.

I cut off his cries with the fire of my engine, and left them standing at the gate as I screamed along the smooth road toward the house.

They were fools.

She was mine. No one could take her from me. Not even her own blood.

CHAPTER NINE
STELLA

I STAYED IN my room for the rest of the day. There was nowhere I could run, nothing to do. I took a long, hot shower. While I'd been out for breakfast—and the run across the lawn, and the nude exhibition—someone had come in and put luxurious shampoos, soaps, and other thoughtful amenities in my bathroom. The mental image of Farns daintily stacking tampon boxes actually pulled a laugh from me. So, that was something.

After my shower I lay on my bed, cooling off, wearing just a towel around my hair. I clicked on the overhead fan with the remote from the bedside table, letting the cool air waft down over me. The quilts along the walls ruffled with the breeze.

I was warm, relatively well fed, and had a modicum of safety in this room. It didn't erase my unease as much as I would have liked. I was still caught in a web, even if the silken threads that bound me were soft and beautiful.

My eyelids drooped, the heat from the shower and the run from the morning pulling me downward into sleep. But I wouldn't go. Whenever my eyes finally closed, I saw Vinemont's face. His anger. And something else, too. The heat when he'd been on top of me in the grass, his hand between my thighs.

I knew it was a transgression. I shouldn't have wanted it. His voice was a subtle poison, creeping into my system, luring me deeper into his hell. My nipples pearled as I remembered the feel of his hard shaft against my thigh. *What would it feel like inside me?*

I tried to swat the thought out of my mind, but my fingers crept down to my still damp pussy. I teased my hard clit with the tip of my finger, sending a jolt of need pulsing through my body. I tried to pull my fingers away, hating the image of Vinemont in my mind, looming over me, his mouth cruel and sensual.

How much of him was covered in the vine tattoos? How low did the ink go?

My finger disobeyed, dipping lower, swirling around my aching clit. My hips rocked up to meet each stroke, the tension rising like someone slowly pulling a string taut. My breaths came in quick pants as I continued working myself, visions of Vinemont's face between my legs driving me wild with the need for release. When I imagined his eyes lit with desire for me and only me, I couldn't hold back the wave of pleasure. I bit my cheek to keep from crying out, though I still made some high-pitched noises that couldn't be mistaken for anything else.

Something slammed somewhere nearby in the house, like a heavy book falling from a high shelf. Embarrassment and worry cooled my brief, blissful high. I whipped the blanket over my body. After a few moments, my breathing returned to normal. I wasn't sated exactly, but I had cleared my head enough to remember that Vinemont was my enemy, nothing more.

I began to drift into sleep when there was a knock at my door. I sat up and glanced to the closet where my few clothes were hanging.

"It's just me, miss." A woman's voice.

"Oh, come in?" I didn't know who 'me' was, but she

sounded harmless enough.

She entered, a middle aged woman in an understated maid's uniform, black except for the white Peter Pan collar. Her hair was strikingly dark, cascading down her back in a shiny mane. If there were any grays, I couldn't see them. She could have been no older than 45.

She smiled, warm and friendly, despite a distinct look of sadness written in the wrinkles around her dark eyes. "Welcome. I'll be your personal maid during your stay with us. If you need anything, just ask for me. I'm Renee."

"So you're the one who put all the good soaps and things in the bathroom?"

"Yes, ma'am. I also took the liberty of ordering some more clothing items in your sizes. Of course, Mr. Sinclair assisted me in choosing for you."

I frowned. The thought of Vinemont choosing my clothes was beyond irritating. I wasn't his pet or a doll he could dress. I was a prisoner.

She folded her hands in front of her. "I know how you feel. It's all more than a little off-putting, but things will fall together in time."

I pulled the towel from my head and rubbed my temple with one hand, the other still holding up the blanket. "You know how I feel? Are you a slave, Renee?"

Her deep brown eyes lit for just a hint of a moment. "I am not, ma'am."

"Then I don't think you could possibly know how I feel. No offense."

"None taken, ma'am." Her gracious smile returned despite my barb.

I sighed. I'd been an Acquisition for less than a day and parts of me—the kind ones, the gentle ones—were already splintering. "I'm sorry," I said as she retreated to my bathroom. "This isn't your fault."

I was the one who signed the contract. Renee didn't force me into it.

She came back with a brush and sat down on the bed

next to me. "Here." She put her hands out, offering to brush my hair.

I scooted around to her, still keeping the blanket pressed to my chest.

"It's fine. I'd be more surprised if you weren't angry." She started at the ends of my hair just like my mother used to do. *"The path of least resistance"* Mom used to call it, working out the kinks from the bottom up until my hair was smooth.

"How many of me have there been?"

She kept brushing with careful strokes. "How many Acquisitions?"

"Yes."

"I'm not sure if I'm supposed to say."

I sighed and let my chin fall to my chest.

She dropped her voice to a whisper. "Two that I know of in the Vinemont family in the past twenty years. There were more before that, but I don't know all the details."

"So few? It isn't an annual sort of thing?"

"No, ma'am."

"You said 'in the Vinemont family'? Are there Acquisitions in other families or something?"

"Yes."

"But why? What's the purpose?" Why would they do this? What could possibly be the reason for enslaving people just for the sake of enslaving them? Maybe that would be the best outcome—a kept slave for a year. No labor, no punishments, no ill treatment. I shook my head. It was all too good to be true. Fear crept up my spine as my question lingered in the air. Something told me there was more, far more to all of it than I could even guess.

"Just tell me why." My tone had gone from curious to desperate.

She hesitated, the brush in the middle of my locks. "You'll see tomorrow."

"What's tomorrow?" Dread settled like an anchor in my gut.

The brush continued, smoothing the waves as it went. "The Acquisition Ball."

Lucius and Vinemont had spoken about a ball over breakfast, but I hadn't realized I would be going.

"A ball? I'm a slave and I'm going to a ball?"

"I really can't say any more."

My mind was whirling. What was this ball? Was it the actual reason, however twisted, for Vinemont to have forced me into the contract?

She reached the crown of my head, still easing the bristles down through the strands. "There, I think we're done."

She rose and then stopped, noticing the photo of my mother and me on my nightstand. "She's beautiful."

I nodded. "She was."

"Your mother?"

"Yes." I studied the picture right along with Renee. I'd been trying for years to divine what she was thinking, why she would leave my father and me the way she did. I supposed I shouldn't have looked too hard, especially given that I'd done the same thing. I just didn't see it all the way through the way she had.

"I'm sorry." Renee put a comforting hand on my shoulder.

She gave me a light squeeze and returned the brush to the bathroom. "I'll have Laura bring your lunch in fifteen minutes if that's all right. Or you can take it downstairs with Mr. Sinclair and Mr. Luciu—"

"Here is fine." The thought of having to see either of them in the same dining room turned my stomach.

She gave a slight bow and left. I dressed in a t-shirt and some pajama bottoms and sank down on the window seat, letting the sun bathe me in afternoon light. The trees were starting to give away their leaves, a brown and orange carpet amassing at the edges of the grass expanse. I pushed the window open and let the cool breeze rush into the room. It carried the smells of grass and woods and water.

I breathed it in, reminding myself I was alive. Even if my life belonged to another for some ridiculous expanse of time, I was alive and I would fight to stay that way. I ran my hand along the scars on one of my wrists. I wouldn't break. I wouldn't go willingly into darkness. Never again.

I spent the rest of the day in my room. Thankfully, I was able to talk Laura into bringing me a sampling of books from the library downstairs. The books were older, but well worth reading, especially the few bodice rippers she'd found.

I'd wanted to wander around the house and investigate, but I kept getting the mental image of two knights in armor crossing their swords in front of me and blocking my way. More than that, the thought of running into Lucius without anyone else around was a chance I wasn't willing to take.

Vinemont didn't summon or visit me at all, which was a relief. He'd gone into town, apparently, to handle some official district attorney business. *Sure.* I supposed the work of railroading innocent citizens was a constant, thankless job.

When Laura brought my dinner, I asked if she could get me some painting supplies. She promised to make my request to Renee. If I were going to spend all my time hiding in my room, which was my game plan so far, then I would need plenty to keep me occupied.

The night passed without incident or even a hint of Vinemont.

The next morning, I was already up and dressed in a light sweater and jeans when the knock came at my door.

"Come in."

Instead of Farns, it was Renee. She was still dressed in

all black with the white collar, and her dark hair was arranged in flowing waves.

"Good morning, ma'am."

"Morning, Renee. And please call me Stella. What happened to Farns?"

"He's with Mr. Sinclair all day. I'm with you. I hope that's all right." Her gaze dropped to the floor.

"Oh, no, no. I didn't mean it that way at all. I was just curious. I'm happy to see you again."

After the words fell out, I realized they were true. I was happy to have someone to talk to. Maybe I could even call her a friend, such as they were in this new world.

She raised her face, her smile making her luminous in the morning light. "I'm happy to see you, too. I must admit, I asked to be assigned to you as soon as I heard about your arrival."

"Why?"

She put her hands in her skirt pockets. "I just feel like we may have some things in common is all."

"Oh, so you hate Sinclair Vinemont, too?"

She laughed. It was an open, inviting sound that held nothing back. "I certainly don't, and I don't believe you do either."

I leaned back against my bedpost. "Pretty sure I do."

"Well, in any case, you have a big day and an even bigger night. I'm here to help you through all of it."

"You told me about the ball tonight. So, what are we doing today?"

"Getting ready, of course. Mr. Sinclair gave me explicit instructions on how he wants you prepared. He ordered your gown the night you arrived, and he picked out your jewels and accessories with me this morning." She walked to me and took my arm. "You are going to be the most beautiful Acquisition they've ever seen."

I pulled my arm from her grasp, anger rushing through me like a wildfire. "You're excited? About putting Vinemont's property on display before some other loathsome people just like him?"

She returned her hands to her pockets. "I was only trying to…" She shrugged and met my eyes again. "I can't undo the contract. I can't stop the ball or anything else that goes on, but I can help you if you'll let me. I can see you through until the end when your year is up and you can leave. That's all I want to do."

The earnestness of her words struck me like a bolt to my heart. She was right. I had signed the contract and now I was bound to it. If she wanted to help, then I would be wise to let her. I only wished I knew more about the Acquisition. Still, I would take whatever allies I could get.

"I'm sorry, Renee. I'm just…"

Emboldened by my apology, she took my arm again. "I know. Like I said yesterday, I understand. Now, let's get you to the spa."

I almost fell back against the bed. "The spa?"

"Here on the property, of course. Mr. Vinemont called in professionals from all over the country for this. You're going to get the royal treatment."

She pulled me out into the hallway and down the front steps.

"What does this entail, exactly?"

"First, breakfast."

I dug in my heels and stopped despite the angry rumble of my stomach. "I don't want to see them."

"The boys are already out and about today. Don't worry."

"*Boys*? You mean the two sadistic men who live here with their third clueless brother?"

She walked me into the thankfully empty breakfast room. "I've known them since they were wee ones, so I still think of them as boys."

She called for Laura, effectively cutting off my incredulous commentary with the sight of a breakfast tray piled high with deliciousness.

Renee sipped her coffee as I demolished my breakfast.

If she was right about having a big day planned, I certainly had a big enough breakfast to power through it.

I wiped my mouth daintily, though it did nothing to undo my earlier lack of manners.

Renee finished her coffee. "Ready to get started?"

I stood and stretched like a lazy cat. "Lead the way."

"One more thing." She showed me down the hallway, leading me deeper into the house than I'd been as of yet. "You are about to meet some new people. They're outsiders. They wouldn't understand what's going on. It would be best if you told them as little as possible in order to avoid any unpleasant complications. They know you're going to a ball. Just keep it at that."

"So I shouldn't tell them that I'm an Acquisition and utterly at the mercy of Vinemont?"

Her quick step faltered for a second but then she regained her pace. "Exactly."

The spa was in a wing toward the back of the house. It was in what seemed to be a converted sunroom. The walls and ceiling were made of paned glass, letting in natural light and warmth. It was an open area with river stone floors, a sunken hot tub in the center of the room, a large wood sauna set to one side, and massage tables to the other. It smelled wonderful, like expensive bath oils and some sort of woodsy incense.

Two men and two women stood waiting for us. Renee went in first and introduced me down the row of staff.

"This is Alex. He's from New Orleans. He'll be in charge of your hair and makeup for the night."

He was a young man with a bright orange faux hawk, multiple piercings in his eyebrows, peacock-colored eyeshadow, and colorful tattoos on each arm.

"Nice to meet you, Ms. Rousseau. When I'm done, you are going to be the belle of the ball."

I looked at Renee, my eyebrows high. "Does everyone know about the ball but me?"

Alex placed a well-manicured hand on my arm. "Oh no, honey. I had to sign a non-disclosure agreement longer than my di—um, longer than my arm, just to get this job, and I still have no idea what you're up to." He winked. "I just know that whatever it is, you are going to look fabulous."

Renee moved me along to the next person. "This is Juliet. She'll be buffing your skin and doing your nails."

"Buffing my skin?"

"Gets rid of all the dead skin cells, makes your skin look like an 18-year-old's." She ran her fingers down my neck and peered at me almost scientifically. "Doesn't look like you've gotten much sun. Perfect. I'll have you shined up like a new penny." She took my hands in hers and examined my nails. They were permanently stained various colors from my paints.

She frowned, her blonde bob falling against her plump cheek as she surveyed the damage. "These will take some work. We may need to use gel to cover the staining."

"Okay I guess?" I'd never really paid much attention to things like my fingernails.

She flipped my hands over and pushed up my sleeves, inspecting further. When she saw the scars along my wrists, she dropped my hands.

Her light blue eyes found mine. "Oh, I'm sorry."

"It's fine. That was a long time ago." I didn't know these people. Still, they were people, and like Renee, they seemed to want to help me. I smiled at her. "It doesn't bother me. You can look at them."

She reclaimed my wrists and ran her fingers over the raised skin. "I think I may have a few tricks to make these less noticeable." She returned my smile, seemingly at ease again.

The next woman had dark hair, a unibrow, and was by far the shortest person in the room.

"Yong will do your waxing."

I whipped my head around to Renee. "Wait, waxing?"

Yong nodded and put a hand on my shoulder, pulling me down so she could inspect my face. "Brows need work...lip looks okay...I'll do full face anyway. Everything else looks fine. When's the last time you had a Brazilian?"

My thighs clenched together involuntarily. "The wax? Never. I don't generally wax anything."

Yong frowned, her unibrow like a dark caterpillar encroaching on her eyes. "I can tell. This will take some work. When I'm done, you'll be smooth as a baby everywhere."

"Um, thanks, I guess?"

She grinned. "I'll go start getting everything ready. It's going to sting some, but you'll love the results."

She passed through an adjoining door, walking quickly and with purpose.

"And this is Dmitri." Renee introduced me to the last person in the row. He stood almost seven feet tall and seemed built of pure muscle. His head was shaved, though dark hair obviously grew there in abundance. He took my hand, his beefy palm swallowing mine whole.

"Very nice to meet you." His Russian accent was so thick it made his words almost unintelligible. But like the others, he had a smile and warmth for me. I appreciated any compassion they had to offer.

"And what do you do, Dmitri?"

He released my hand and held his palms in front of me. "Massage."

"Oh." I swallowed hard.

"I no hurt you." He squeezed my hand encouragingly. "Well, maybe a little. You like. Promise."

"First, into the hot tub," Juliet said. "I need your skin nice and pruny." She stepped toward the massage tables. "Come on, get on in. We have a lot to do."

"You want me to just strip in front of everyone?" I looked from Renee to Juliet and then up at Dmitri.

I crossed my arms over my chest. They could clean me up and dress me like a doll, but I wasn't going to run around naked for their amusement.

Dmitri laughed, the sound filling the large room and making it seem somehow small. "Nothing new to me, Miss Stella. But I wait over there if make you more comfortable." He shrugged and went through the same door as Yong.

"Needless to say, this"—Alex waved his hand up and down at my body—"does nothing for me. But I'll still be a gentleman and wait in my booth. I'm going to need to send out for a bit more color, anyway. I'm thinking we're going to make your red a bit more strawberry and maybe a touch of…" His words trailed off as he left the room.

Renee backed up and took a seat near the door before pulling a small book from her pocket. "I'll stay with you in case you need anything. Just try to relax. Enjoy it. Mr. Sinclair has spared no expense."

"First class ticket from L.A. and a sweet paycheck," Juliet agreed.

I smirked. "Well, we definitely want Vinemont to get his money's worth." I stripped without ceremony and stepped into the bubbling water in the center of the room.

"I met him for all of five seconds. That man is absolutely dreamy." Juliet knelt in a corner of the room and began removing various equipment from a large rolling case.

Was she going to use all that on me?

"Yeah, if you like tall, dark, and psychotic," I said.

Renee snorted.

I slid further down into the enveloping warmth, and lay my head back.

"So are you really going to a ball?" Juliet asked.

"That's what I keep hearing."

Juliet squealed a little. "That's just so, so exciting! And

like, romantic. We don't do stuff like balls in L.A.—I should have been born Southern. I wish I could go with you."

"No, you don't." I closed my eyes and let my whispered words fade into the bubbling heat around me.

Four hours later, I was putty in Dmitri's strong hands. I lay completely naked—my sense of modesty waxed away right along with all my body hair—and let his magical fingers work me over.

"You so tense, *Krasivaya.*" Dmitri had taken to referring to me as krasivaya. I didn't know what it meant and I honestly didn't care as long as he kept smoothing his hands over my body and making my muscles sing.

I'd been buffed, oiled, manicured, pedicured, handfed by Renee as my nails dried, and now I was being turned into a limp noodle by Dmitri.

"It's almost my turn. I can't wait." Alex clapped his hands as he stood next to me. "You know, I've never really cared for the female form, but I might make an exception for yours. It's actually pretty. If you had a dick, I'd definitely fuck you."

I snickered as Dmitri's large palm pressed into my lower back.

"Why so many girl-men in this country? In Russia, we have no such men. Only real men." Dmitri moved to my ass and rubbed from there down to my thighs in strong strokes, as if squeegeeing my stress away.

"Is that so? I have an ex-boyfriend who came straight from Russia with man love. That St. Petersburg boy could power bottom like a son of a bitch."

"Truly?" Dmitri squeezed and rolled my thighs.

"I had the orgasms to prove it."

I moaned as Dmitri's hands worked the tension from me. Had I been afraid of him? He was a massage god.

"Ah, hear that? That is what real men desire to hear. To make woman tremble with desire for him. You need to learn this. Then you be real man."

"Yeah, I'll get right to work on that." Alex patted my behind. "You're mine next. And I promise, unlike some *real men*"—he mimicked a Russian accent—"I won't have a raging boner when I'm touching you."

I giggled. I didn't care if Dmitri was jacking off all over me, just so long as he kept pushing my tension all the way down my body and out my toes. I'd gotten massages before, but nothing compared to this. Not even close.

"How's the Acquisition doing?"

Lucius' voice undid Dmitri's work and made my muscles seize.

Dmitri must have felt the change because he let out a litany in angry Russian. His hands rested possessively on my lower back as Lucius leisurely made his way to me. Whereas Vinemont was a methodical serial killer, Lucius was more of a smooth assassin. His fluid movements and swimmer's body hinted at quickness and wiry strength.

Renee stood and pocketed her book, but didn't move.

I couldn't get up, because Lucius would see me fully naked. His seeing only my ass, once again, seemed like the lesser of two evils.

"Krasivaya doesn't like you, comrade. You interfere with her pleasure." Dmitri's voice was a cautionary rumble.

Lucius stopped next to me, his black boots filling my vision. "I'm certain that's not so. I could give her plenty more pleasure if we had this room all to ourselves."

"Well, you don't." Dmitri stepped around the table and stood chest to chest with Lucius.

"What, because you're here? A hired set of hands?" Lucius placed his hand on my ass and squeezed.

I tried to jerk away from him, but I had nowhere to go. Dmitri yanked Lucius' hand away from me. I scrambled off the table and backed away from them, nudity be damned.

Dmitri and Lucius faced off against each other, neither man backing down.

Lucius smiled up at Dmitri, as if declaring a truce with the bigger man. Instead of walking away, Lucius struck quickly with a vicious haymaker across Dmitri's jaw. A classic sucker punch. Dmitri staggered back. Rage lit the Russian's face and he swung, catching Lucius on the chin and sending him reeling away. Instead of falling, Lucius seemed emboldened and charged the larger man.

Juliet and Alex each came to either side of me.

"Now this is entertainment," Alex said. "I wish they hadn't confiscated my cell. I'd post a vid of this hunk on hunk action and make a fortune."

"Lucius!" Vinemont rushed into the room. He saw me and stopped, his mouth opening slightly.

I slung an arm across my breasts and crossed my legs, though it didn't do much good. I was completely bare down there now, with nothing left to the imagination.

Lucius turned and looked at me too, his signature lascivious smile returning to his otherwise handsome face. Dmitri took the opportunity to get him in a headlock. They struggled against each other, Lucius trying to buck Dmitri's vice-like hold around his neck. Lucius shoved an elbow back hard into Dmitri's ribs, breaking the Russian's hold and slipping away.

Vinemont appeared to come back to himself and darted between the two men. "Lucius, get the hell out of here!"

"This is my house, too, Sin," Lucius said. "I can go wherever the fuck I want. We're brothers, remember?" He glanced over his shoulder at me. "We share."

"Not this we don't," Vinemont growled.

"We'll see." Lucius dragged his thumb across his chin, wiping the blood from his split lip. He squared off against Dmitri again. "You hit pretty good for a red."

"You hit pretty good for a *devushka*."

"*Ya yebat' etu devochku pryamo pered vami*," Lucius replied with a matching accent. He glanced over at me again.

Dmitri took a threatening step forward, menace oozing from his pores.

I wanted Dmitri to smash Lucius to a bloody pulp, to wipe the self-satisfied grin from his face.

Vinemont pushed each man backward. "Stop!"

"Is it hot in here? It definitely feels hot in here." Alex used his hand as a fan.

"Agreed." Juliet's hand was at her throat as she watched the men, her tongue darting at the corners of her mouth.

Vinemont jabbed a finger into his brother's chest. "Lucius, I'm warning you. Get out."

"You aren't the Sovereign. Stop acting like you are."

Vinemont advanced on Lucius until both men were almost nose to nose.

"Stand down, Lucius."

The staring competition lasted for a few tense moments before Lucius blinked and backed away. "I didn't know you'd get your panties so bunched over an Acquisition. I should have. You've always been a royal cockblock."

Lucius sauntered toward the exit before glancing over his shoulder. "See you around, Stella."

Alex let out a bated breath. "I want to see him around. More accurately, I want to see my mouth around his—"

"Stella, for Christ's sake, cover yourself." Vinemont didn't move and kept his gaze trained on me.

Yong bustled in from the waxing room—or as I called it, the room of intense pain and humiliation—and tossed me a towel. I grabbed it and wrapped it around myself so fast I almost dropped it.

Vinemont watched every single movement, as if he were attuned to me on some primitive level. He blinked slowly and scrubbed a hand down his face. "How much longer before she's ready?"

"Three hours," Alex said.

"Have her ready in two. The seamstress should be here any minute to fit her. I don't want any delays."

"Stop talking about me like I'm not here."

Vinemont turned his wrathful gaze back to me. "Fine. Be ready in two hours. If you disappointment me, there will be a high price to pay and *you* will pay it."

He turned on his heel and left, fury in his steps.

"That. Was. Intense." Alex leaned on the massage table. "I kind of want to make you late just so you get some sort of naughty punishment. Sweet Jesus, do I want some BDSM lovin' right about now."

Juliet sagged with relief. "Both of those hotties want to get with you. You know that, right?"

"That first one does not deserve to even look at you, much less enjoy your kiska." Dmitri's face darkened anew with anger.

"Don't worry," I said, "my kiska is mine alone, if I take your meaning. By the way, what did Lucius say to you in Russian?"

I didn't think it was possible, but Dmitri's glower deepened. "He is, how you say, confident your kiska will be his."

"Well." Alex took my hand. "I may not have a taste for kiska, but if we only have two hours, you're mine, sugar."

Dmitri grumbled about not finishing the massage, and promised he would be back to take care of me.

Alex plopped me into his chair and got to work. He was a madman with scissors and chemicals that smelled like a mix of turpentine and overripe fruit. He foiled, heated, rinsed, and cut, turning my scalp into a beauty battleground. My hair was still the same red, but with highlights and lowlights to set off the color. He put it up in big hot rollers and sprayed it down with an obscene amount of hairspray.

He then set about to do my makeup. I was a bit

worried, given the peacock colors above his eyes and his bright lips. He made it worse by not letting me look into the mirror until he was done. After what felt like over an hour of brushing, shadowing, highlighting, contouring, and coloring, I finally got a chance to see the finished product.

"Voila!" He whirled me around and held the swivel chair steady before the mirror.

I'd never thought of myself as a ten. I was self-aware enough to know I was pretty by most standards, but nothing about me said movie star or model. When I looked at what Alex had done, there was more than just a tinge of amazement in my stare. He'd highlighted my high cheekbones and plump lips. He'd given me dramatic eyebrows with a killer arch. Most of all, he'd brought out the deep green color of my eyes. They'd never looked so bright.

"Wow," was all I could muster.

"Wow is right, honey. That right there is the money shot. That face, that hair. One in a million, trust me." He smiled back at me from the mirror.

Renee walked in and clasped her hands in front of her. "This is... You are... I've never..." It ended in no words but a high pitched gleeful sound.

The reserved maid looked positively girlish. "You are absolute perfection."

"Why, thank you." Alex gave a small bow.

I laughed. I was beginning to enjoy my ragtag band of beauty assistants. I tried not to think about how I may never see them again after today. It was hard to think of a reason why Vinemont would send for them again. I couldn't imagine going to too many balls. In fact, I had a suspicion that this "ball" was quite a bit more than it seemed.

It didn't matter what it was. I would go. I would do what I had to so that my father would remain free and alive. There was no going back, only forward. And forward meant I had to get through the ball and the 363 days thereafter.

"The seamstress is outside." Renee calmed herself and motioned for me to rejoin the others in the main room.

The seamstress was an economical woman in a pantsuit and flats, chalk in her fingers and a pencil behind her ears. What she'd brought me to wear wasn't practical in the least. It was perched on a model form. I had never seen anything like it short of the pages in fashion magazines. It was a deep green gown with a plunging neckline, lace straps, and a ball gown skirt made entirely of black peacock feathers.

Alex gasped and ran to the gown. "Oh my god, oh my god. I have never seen anything as fabulous in all my years and, trust me, I've seen more than my fair share of fabulous things. Who's the designer and when can I have one?"

"I designed it and, I assure you, it's a one of a kind." The seamstress eyed me. I got the distinct feeling she was somehow taking my measurements through my towel. She quirked up a corner of her lip, as if pleased. "I think it should be an almost perfect fit with a few tucks here and there."

Alex was gushing as I gaped at the dress. It was extravagant, over-the-top. I wanted to sketch it, not wear it.

Renee walked around the garment, examining it with a hyper-critical eye. I couldn't imagine what a woman who dressed in plain black, wore no makeup, and seemed to do nothing to pretty herself in the least could find lacking in the dream creation before her.

"I think you are very close, Enid." Renee tapped her finger on her chin. "Where's the vine detail?"

"Her cloak." Enid snapped her fingers and what seemed like a harried assistant rushed in, glasses askew, pushing a wheeled mannequin ahead of her. It was covered in a black cloak with embroidered deep green vines twining all around the material.

"And her jewels." Enid motioned the assistant closer. She held a red velvet box under her arm.

Enid took it and undid the delicate clasp, opening the box and blinding me with sparkle. Inside lay a silver necklace with emeralds arranged in the same vine motif. A pair of large emerald earrings completed the set.

Renee's eyes brightened when she saw the fantastic jewels. "I haven't seen these for twenty years." She reached a hand out, as if to touch them, but simply held it above the priceless array.

Enid clapped her hands. "Well, we're burning daylight. Drop the towel, let's get you dressed."

I shifted from one foot to the next. "Did you bring underwear? I'll need to go to my room to get some before I can put all this on."

Enid put her hands on her hips. "Do you think I'm going to let you ruin my splendid gown with some bunchy cotton panties?"

I put a matching hand on my hip. "I can't go to a ball commando, now can I?"

"You can and you will."

"What?"

"Strip." Enid's mouth was set in a firm line.

"Do it, do it, do it!" Alex tried to yank the towel off me. "I have to see it in motion. It may kill me from fashion overload, but I'll die happy."

I glanced over at Dmitri. He sighed, as if hoping I'd forgotten he was there. "Fine, fine. I won't watch. Even though you let girl-man see." He frowned at Alex and turned his back.

I finally let Alex tug the towel free and stepped toward the feathery cloud.

CHAPTER TEN
SINCLAIR

WHERE IS SHE? I waited out in front of the house in a black sports car. I was too on edge to even bother with my usual driver. I needed control any way I could get it.

Going to the Acquisition Ball was something I had never done before. All the preparation in the world likely wouldn't ready me for what was about to happen. I would get through it. Making sure Stella performed—that she stood out—was my main goal. I gripped the steering wheel, trying to decide if I needed to go inside and drag her out, when the front door opened.

Renee stepped out first, and then I saw her. The late afternoon sun blinked off the jewels at her throat, barely visible above the dark cloak tied at her neck. Her dress was the signature Vinemont green, and Enid had outdone herself on the skirt. The black peacock feathers would turn more than a few heads. I only hoped one of them belonged to the Sovereign.

If that weren't enough, Stella's face was radiant. Even as she crossed the threshold, uncertainty painting her features, she made something inside me click into a higher gear. Her bright green gaze tried to ensnare me, tried to make me feel something. I didn't. I wouldn't.

Still, I wanted to see her—all of her. Damn that cloak. I imagined ripping it all off her except the jewels, and my cock thickened in my tuxedo pants. *Fuck*. Now was neither the time nor the place.

It was going to take everything I had to get through this night. It was going to take even more out of Stella. Once it was all over, she wouldn't want to have anything to do with me. She probably already felt that way after what had happened in the yard yesterday. Tonight would seal the deal. Not that she'd have any choice. She would do as I told her. She cared about her father too damned much not to.

She wore a pair of breakneck high heels. I imagined how long her legs would look, bare and smooth, wearing nothing but her stilettos. I shifted in my seat. The large Russian walked out the door behind her and helped her down the front steps. He smiled easily as she spoke to him. I wanted to destroy him for even thinking of talking to what was mine, to take him down and show her I could do it. I could hurt, kill. I could do even worse.

She took the last few steps to my car, and the Russian bastard had the nerve to open the door for her. She maneuvered into the tight space, tucking her dress in and almost falling into the seat.

"Easy *krasivaya*," he said.

A muscle ticked in my jaw as he called her beautiful. She was my pet. If anyone were to give her a special name in Russian or any other fucking language, it would be me.

"I see you when you return." He closed the door and moved away from the car.

No, you won't. I put the car in reverse and backed away from the house. Lucius stood in one of the downstairs windows and watched us leave. Actually, he didn't watch *us*, his gaze was fixed on Stella.

"He creeps me out." Her eyes were trained on the same window.

"Don't talk about my brother like that." He was blood. She was an Acquisition. Even if I wanted to beat the desirous look out of his eyes until all I saw was gore, some bonds were unbreakable.

"Fine." She sank back in the seat as far as she could and stared out the window. I glanced at her, taking in her stunning profile. Creamy, smooth skin, delicate nose, sumptuous pout... Her lips were painted a blood red, the perfect complement to the emeralds at her throat.

I wore classic black tie. I didn't need to stand out. I was nothing more than background noise. Stella was the attraction, the star.

We fell into an uncomfortable silence as I cycled the gears, sped through the estate, and maneuvered out onto the road. The ball was held at the Oakman estate, and had been for as long as anyone cared to remember. This year's affair promised to be even more extravagant than previous years, given that Cal Oakman was the current Sovereign.

The bastard was revered throughout our community. His winning Acquisition ten years ago had cemented him at the top of Louisiana society. I hadn't attended that ball, despite the engraved platinum invitation. Now I wished I had. At least I would know more of what to expect. Hopefully my mother's recollections of her Acquisition Ball twenty years ago would still hold true. They should. Tradition and ritual were the bedrock principles beneath the entire system.

"What's going to happen?"

I ignored her question. If I described what I expected to go on at the ball, she might put up enough fight to be a problem. I needed her just as she was, a perfectly tantalizing morsel, wide-eyed and beautiful. I needed her eventual downfall to be spectacular. I needed to win.

Twilight fell as we sped along country roads, past vast estates hidden behind walls of trees and dark bayous.

"I won't run." Her voice was quiet, but resolute.

"What?" I downshifted as we came closer to the

Oakman gate.

"If you tell me what's going to happen, I won't run. I know there's nowhere to go and you'll hurt my father if I do. So, just tell me."

I pulled the car over so quickly she yelped. The freshly fallen leaves crunched under the tires as we skidded to a halt.

"You want to know what the most powerful people in the South, maybe the entire fucking country, are going to do to you tonight?"

She winced and then turned her wide, angry eyes to me. "Yes."

"Remember how I said I would hurt you?"

"Yes."

"Tonight, I won't be the only one inflicting the pain. That's all you need to know."

I wanted to be the only one to hurt her, the only one to make her cry or bleed or scream. Instead, Cal fucking Oakman would be sharing the duties, and for an audience. She was mine—not because I cared about her, but because I owned her.

I hit the steering wheel and turned to her, pinching her chin between my thumb and forefinger. "You just have to get through it. No matter what happens."

Her breaths came faster and she leaned toward me, her cloak falling to the side and revealing the swells of her breasts. "But you'll be there? With me?"

She was drawing me toward her somehow until my lips were only a whisper away from hers. She smelled like rosewater and honey, a scent I'd chosen for her for the evening. It was meant to be intoxicating, to draw people in, but it wasn't supposed to work against me like this. Her eyes closed, her lips in full bloom and ready for a kiss.

Once again, I was letting my family down. She was property. I needed to stop acting like she was anything more than that. But she didn't make it easy. The day before when she'd lain on her bed and stroked herself, making quiet cries and grinding her hips against her hand, it took every ounce of willpower I possessed not to burst into her room and fuck her until she screamed my name. The memory went straight to my dick, making a bad situation even worse.

Her question came back to me. Would I be there with her? Yes. Would she be happy about it? No. Definitely not. Her lips begged for solace I could not and would not give. I pulled away and made a show of wiping my fingers on my handkerchief.

"You must be desperate if you think I offer you any more safety than the strangers you're about to meet. I don't."

She recoiled, stung by my words, by my actions. Good. She needed to hate me. It would make it all easier.

I put the car back into gear and pulled from the shoulder. I was desperate to get out of this enclosed space, away from her eyes, her scent, her lips, her breath.

As I wished for an escape, the wide gates of the Oakman estate loomed ahead of us. Several cars passed through after their occupants showed the guards the distinctive engraved invitation—this year's was solid gold. I hefted the plate from my inner coat pocket and flashed it before I was waved through to the tree-lined lane. The Oakman home rose from the landscape, a French chateau built in the style of Versailles. Stella took a deep, steadying breath beside me. Nervousness? Excitement? Dread? Any one of those, or all at once, maybe.

I mimicked her quietly, trying to calm my nerves right along with hers. So much was riding on this. On her. She would either save the Vinemonts or break us. Tonight was her first step toward either destiny.

CHAPTER ELEVEN
STELLA

THE HOUSE IN the oak grove was ominous despite the fact that the outside was lit up as bright as day. Ballgoers climbed the wide stone stairs to the open and bright front entrance. I shivered.

I'd almost had him only moments before, but the iota of control I wielded over Vinemont wasn't enough. My lips, my words, none of it was enough to make him change his course. I entertained the ridiculous fantasy that if I could get him to care about me, then he wouldn't hurt me. I knew he wouldn't let me go, not until the year was up. But maybe I could convince him to leave me alone, to let me paint, to let me do anything besides standing naked for his amusement or enduring any of his cruel intentions.

But then he'd pulled away, becoming his usual cold self. At the last moment, I'd lost him.

Even though I hadn't been able to shake him, whatever lay within the chateau put Vinemont on edge. I didn't think anything could make him nervous. He tried to hide it beneath his usual snobby veneer, but I saw it clearly. He could hide plenty from me, but not that. Even he didn't look forward to the dark deeds that awaited in this place.

He pulled up to a valet. For the first time, I noticed all of the people walking past the car were wearing masks. I turned back to Vinemont to find he'd already donned a simple black mask covered with the vine motif, his blue eyes showing through the material like patches of dark sky. His jaw was tight, the clean shaven lines perfection beneath his disguise. He pulled a far more extravagant mask from behind my seat, made with the same black peacock feathers on my dress.

"Put it on."

I slipped the ribbons around my head and tied them in the back. Alex would have had a fit if he had seen me so much as touch my hair. I felt a pang in my breast at the thought of never seeing my short-lived friends again. After Mom had died, I didn't do much besides keep my father company, paint, and read. I had no friends to speak of, no one to notice I was gone.

Now that I didn't belong to myself anymore, I realized what a sheltered, useless existence I'd truly had. I was utterly unprepared for the world, for Vinemont, for the shadows that threatened to smother the very life from my body. I could feel it, the darkness, swirling near me, taking the air from my lungs like a greedy parasite.

The valet had been holding his hand out for an awkward moment before I took it and allowed him to help me from the car. He wore a silver mask with what looked like an oak branch pattern in stark black lines.

"Thank you."

"My pleasure," the valet said. "Welcome to the Oakman chateau."

"Not a scratch." Vinemont threw the keys. The valet caught them easily.

Vinemont came around and offered his arm to me. I would have refused had it not been for the too-high heels strapped to my feet. As it was, I would need help climbing the wide stairs unless I wanted to break my neck.

I pushed my cloak out of the way and took his arm. Warmth radiated from him, seeping through his tuxedo and into my bare arm. With the shoes, I was tall enough to get a good look at his face, despite the mask hiding him from me. His jaw was tight, stress written in the tension.

We began our climb as others crowded around us. I tried to listen to the snippets of conversation.

"—picked this year?"

"I heard the same thing! Cal is apparently very interested in the new Acquisitions to the point he—"

"I hope the Witheringtons win. Have you seen their eldest? He's still a bachel—"

The blood drained from my face. The tips of my ears went cold. I stopped even as Vinemont tried to tug me along with him. "This is some sort of sick competition?"

A couple of masked people near us turned to look.

"Her first ball," Vinemont said cheerily.

"Oh, my dear, you're in for a real treat!" A female ballgoer in a sparkling mask with a grotesquely long nose took my other arm.

She and Vinemont walked me up the stairs.

"This year is going to be especially interesting," the beast at my other elbow trilled. "The three families are really the crème de la crème. Top notch. And Cal is going to be the greatest master of ceremonies we've ever seen if his Acquisition was any indication. He really set the bar high that year. Have you heard what he has planned for tonight?"

"Don't spoil it for her," Vinemont said with a smile in his voice. "I want her to get the full experience."

I cursed him silently for cutting off my only flow of information.

We reached the top step and fell in line behind some other couples.

"In that case, I'll say no more. See you inside. I'll tell you one thing, though, this year's Acquisitions are going to be much the worse for wear when it's over." With that, she giggled and rejoined her party.

I faltered, my heel catching as the corners of my vision darkened. Blood roared in my ears. Vinemont held me up and wrapped his arm around my waist, pulling me into his side.

"Keep it together, Stella." His voice was low.

"Just tell me what's going to happen." Desperation colored my words, only hinting at the panic escalating in my breast.

He continued moving me inexorably forward. Panic rose up from within me, threatening to overtake the thin veneer of control I had. I wanted to scream, to run, to do anything but go inside this house with the monster at my elbow.

"Please, Sinclair, please."

He stiffened as I used his first name. He pulled me to the side and let others pass ahead of us.

"Goddammit, Stella." His voice was a low growl as his eyes flashed behind the black mask. "Stop asking questions. In fact, don't speak again until you're spoken to. Understand?"

"I'll stop and I won't speak if you just answer my question. Just tell me."

He brought me closer to him, pretending we were embracing each other, solely for the benefit of the other ballgoers around us, no doubt.

His mouth was at my ear. "I haven't told you for a reason, Stella."

He put a hand to my throat before smoothing it around to the back of my neck in a move of utter possession.

"They will mark you." He ran his fingers across the skin at the nape of my neck, making a vivid heat tear through my body from the points of contact. "Here."

His other hand snaked under my cloak and around to the open back of my dress. His fingers played at my exposed skin. "And here."

I shook so hard that he spread his large palm against my bare back and pressed me to him. "I warned you, Stella. I didn't want you to know ahead of time. Fear is your enemy. Fear will make it hurt more than it has to. Now, look at you." He slid his hand up my spine. "Trembling against me, the one who stole you away from your life, the one who's going to take everything from you. You are cozying up to the spider you detest."

His lips brushed my earlobe and the strange heat pulsed through me again, scorching a path straight to my core. His evil words weren't igniting fear in me. They were making me need him, need his wicked tongue to do things other than taunt me with pain.

I knew I should be afraid. I was. But not of him.

He moved his hand around to the front of my dress and teased my hardened nipple with his thumb. He groaned low in his throat. The cloak hid his movements, but I felt every single touch. When he cupped my breast and squeezed, I hitched in my breath.

"You'd let me fuck you right now, wouldn't you? In front of all these people. Right here." He released my nape, grabbed my hand, and guided it to the hard length in his pants. "You'd take this."

My heart fluttered even faster. I slid my hand along him and his hips jerked toward me. I couldn't think, couldn't waste my thoughts on fear when he created an inferno that scorched me in my most secret places.

"Yes," I breathed. "I would."

"And I'd take you, too. In fact, I will, but not here. Business first. Get through this, and I'll grant you a reward." With that, he let me go and backed away. His step was steady but his eyes were wild.

My skin was needy, demanding his touch and more. What was wrong with me? I *hated* Vinemont. Maybe it was because of what I'd done to myself. Maybe I felt like I deserved some sort of punishment for being so weak throughout my life? I didn't know. All I knew was that I wanted him to rekindle the same fire in me, to make me burn for him, no matter the cost.

He held out his arm for me again. I took it and allowed him to escort me into the glowing hell of the Oakman chateau.

Masked greeters welcomed us and offered to take my cloak. Vinemont declined and swept me further inside the mansion. It was alight with conversation and alcohol. Servers in harlequin masks wove through the revelers, offering drinks and taking already empty glasses.

One whisked towards us, his tray laden with champagne.

"No, thank you," I said.

Vinemont grabbed two glasses and handed me one. "Drink. It'll help."

I took a sip and then another. We walked further inside. Everything was gilded, golden, and sparkling. Dozens of chandeliers lined the high ceilings, and the walls were covered with intricate murals of romanticized scenes from the old South. It reflected a whitewashed history, the lighter paint hiding a bloody and violent past.

I waved my glass at the images of cotton fields and smiling slaves. "This is disgusting."

"Thank you for your fascinating art critique. Now, drink," Vinemont urged.

I swallowed another mouthful of the champagne, my stomach warming. And then the delicious liquid was gone. Vinemont handed the second glass to me.

"Finish it."

I did as he instructed, suddenly thirsty and starving. My lunch at Renee's hands seemed to have happened days ago.

"Good." He passed the empty glasses to a particularly

horrific server dressed in complete maudlin. His mask was skeletal even as the bells jingled merrily along his crown.

What sounded like a full orchestra began playing somewhere deeper in the house. Vinemont and I fell into the stream of masked strangers, some of them in gorgeous gowns that seemed to have come right off a runway. The men were all in staid black tie, the only things marking them as different were the varied masks that hid their faces. Some were pure peacocks, others in simple black. All seemed eager, almost excited. A buzz was in the crowd, elation at what came next, whatever that might be, creating an expectant energy.

A man plucked the edge of my cape and stared down at me.

I cringed back into Vinemont.

The stranger didn't seem to notice, or care. "A Vinemont, I take it?"

The hum of the music grew, the whine of violins echoing down the wide marble hallway before the sound coalesced into beauty along with the other instruments.

"Yes." Vinemont pulled me into his side, forcing the stranger to release my cloak.

The stranger smiled, his eyes lighting behind his midnight blue mask. "There are no female Vinemont heirs. So you must be an Acquisition."

"I'm just—"

"She's mine. Back the fuck off, Charles." Vinemont tightened his grip at my waist, pressing the already tight dress into me even more.

The stranger laughed. "Nice to see you, too, Sinclair." He stared down into my eyes again. "And I'm very much looking forward to seeing you, all of you, very shortly."

The floor lurched beneath my feet. The only thing that kept me upright was Vinemont's arm around my waist. He was a prison made of flesh and blood. My very own cage.

The stranger, Charles, stepped away and whispered something to the woman at his side. She frowned at me, giving me an up and down sweep with a critical gaze, her crimson mask turning her into a particularly vicious foe.

The orchestra was playing some elegant tune, one made for the opera or a symphony, not for this. It was so out of place that I wanted to laugh. I stifled my giggle as I glanced away from the crimson bitch.

I ignored the priceless canvases that graced the walls, and the ornate doors and moldings. Instead of letting the beauty of the house lull me, I stared into the masked faces, many of them now staring back at me as word spread that I was an Acquisition, whatever that really meant. Was I so rare? How many Acquisitions were there?

Though light glanced from every surface and sprang from the bright walls and polished floor, I was in a nightmare. The home was only gilded, gold covering the rotten core. I was surrounded by ghouls, all of them hungering for a piece of my flesh. The glitz and glamour did nothing to hide their true natures. No mask ever could.

The quick beat of my heart resounded in my ears, deafening even the smooth sound of the instruments. Vinemont didn't stop, didn't say a word, just kept moving forward. Toward what, I didn't know. We passed through a wide set of high doors and into a ballroom. The floor was a light oak and shone like everything else in the vile mansion.

In the center was a high platform that towered over the ballgoers. It was circular and done in brilliant gold. A fabricated oak tree shot up through the middle, the leaves sprouting artificially green and full almost up to the ceiling, which must have been forty feet overhead, if not more.

Vinemont swept me through the crowd, moving closer to the tree. I wanted to dig in my heels, to stop his resolute forward momentum. It was no use. The nearer we drew to the platform, the louder my instinct screamed for me to run. Something metallic along the trunk caught my eye and my knees almost gave way. Three sets of silver shackles hung from the tree, each attached to chains that ascended into the branches above.

"No." I pushed back against Vinemont.

"Calm down." He changed course and led me around the tree and further toward the orchestra.

Another platform was set up toward the back of the room near the floor-to-ceiling windows. Three men sat atop it, each with a table in front of them at knee level. Each was shirtless. Every bare piece of their muscular skin was covered in ink—naked women, skulls, tribal, even flowers. One in a goblin mask seemed to pick Vinemont and me from the crowd.

"He's staring at us," I said. "The goblin, up there."

"Everyone's staring at us."

Vinemont led me toward the goblin. I didn't want to go, but I didn't want to retreat and get any closer to the tree, either. We stopped midway between the two, far too close to the tree for my liking.

The orchestra suddenly quieted and then the hall fell utterly silent. All masks turned toward the platform where a man stood, his arms outstretched, a microphone in one hand. Someone worked up in the rafters of the hall, training a spotlight down on the apparent star of the show. His mask seemed to be an array of oak leaves, the same that decorated the tree behind him.

"Welcome to the twenty-fifth Acquisition Ball!" he shouted into his microphone.

A cheer went up from the crowd and then they all clapped as if they were at the opening of the Kentucky Derby.

After a ridiculous span of applause, the man held his hands out to quiet crowd.

"This year, we have an amazing slate of competitors." He gazed around at the people beneath him, clearly a showman. "Though, of course, not as amazing as my Acquisition year. Cal Oakman for the win!"

Laughter sounded through the cavernous hall. Vinemont neither clapped nor laughed, just stood with me at his side. Tension was etched in his bearing just as fear must have been etched into mine.

"It has been an honor to be your Sovereign for the past decade, and I am pleased to say that any of the three firstborns chosen for this year's Acquisition will make an excellent addition to the Sovereign legacy I leave behind. And now, without further ado, let's introduce the Acquiring families!"

Another roar from the crowd.

The Acquiring firstborns were *chosen*? Vinemont hadn't volunteered to ruin me, humiliate me? Of course he had. He was a cruel man who enjoyed hurting me. Wasn't he? I couldn't tell what was real anymore. And why were there three? I glanced around. Out of all these masked faces, only two could be my allies.

"First up. Robert Eagleton. Come on up, Bob, and show us what you brought with you!"

Someone moved through the crowd to our right. A middle-aged balding man in an eagle mask led a much larger man wearing a nearly identical mask. They took the stairs to the top of the platform and shared the spotlight with Oakman. The balding man puffed a bit, but the taller, younger man just stood and surveyed the crowd below.

"All right Bob, tell us who we have here." Oakman should have hosted a game show. He held the microphone out for Bob.

"This is, well, this is Gavin. He's my, um, Acquisition. And we will win this year." Bob let out a sigh of relief, as if he'd gotten past the hardest part.

"Ready for the first reveal, everyone?"

Another bloodthirsty cheer. Or maybe the champagne bubbles playing in my mind just thought it was bloodthirsty.

Oakman removed the man's mask. He looked to be in his early twenties, dark eyes, pale skin, short brown hair, handsome even from this distance. The crowd twittered and some wolf whistles rang out.

"Looks like we have a competition." Oakman clapped Bob and Gavin off the stage along with the crowd.

"Up next, the Witheringtons. Red, you out there?"

More cheers.

Another man weaved through the crowd on the opposite side of the platform. He pulled a woman in a feather mask behind him, practically dragging her to the top of the platform.

The man, Red, took the microphone from Oakman. "This is Brianne, this year's winning Acquisition."

Red stripped her mask away, revealing a small, scared blonde. Her eyes were huge, and she visibly quaked under the spotlight.

"Oh, my," Oakman stepped back and gave an over-the-top up and down look. "We've got some stiff competition, if you folks know what I mean!"

Hoots and whistles, mixed with laughter, echoed around the hall.

"We're next." Vinemont's voice was in my ear, each syllable laced with rigid determination. Any hint of the heat he'd shown me outside was gone. He released my waist and took my hand. His palms were damp, the only indication that he was at all nervous.

Brianne and Red retreated from the platform.

"Now, last but never least, the Vinemonts. Counsellor Sinclair, show us your wares!"

He strode forward, confidence in every movement, and pulled me behind him. The tree loomed ahead, the shackles glinting in the spotlight. Foreboding rose inside me and blotted out my voice, my heart, and my soul. I followed. There was nowhere else to go.

We took the stairs one at a time, each step adding a weight to my shoulders, a rock to my stomach. Finally, we stood next to Oakman. Everything beyond the glittering stage was a dark blur. The spotlight was a blinding sun, focused on me as if by a cruel child with a magnifying glass.

"Her name is Stella, not that it matters." Vinemont was cold, his words like frost in my mind.

He untied my mask and yanked it from my face. Then he ripped the cloak from me, my skin tingling from the sudden onslaught of open air. A collective gasp rose up from the crowd, followed by thunderous applause.

"Oh my, my. Now, Sinclair, you know I've always had a thing for redheads. And this is one is too choice to pass up."

"I'll tell you what, Cal, when I'm Sovereign, I'll send you a new redhead each week," Vinemont said to raucous laughter from the crowd below.

"I like the confidence. I've got my eye on this one, ladies and gents. Now, let's get this party started right. Branding time!"

The orchestra started back up and Vinemont pulled me down from the platform. No longer hidden by the ornate mask or my cloak, I felt naked. The ghouls stared and leered as I walked past, Vinemont dragging me along through the pressing bodies.

Wait, *branding time?*

He was leading me toward the tattooed goblin again. The male Acquisition, Gavin, was already shirtless and lying on his stomach, one of the other artists inking him in front of the masked onlookers.

"Bigger," Bob directed.

The artist nodded and continued free-handing the outline of an eagle on Gavin's shoulder blade.

The orchestra changed to a waltz, and many ballgoers paired off to dance, skirts swirling, their laughter melding with the music.

Red led his Acquisition, Brianne, over to one of the tables and shoved her down onto her back. He pulled the strap of her dark purple dress down so her left breast was exposed. "Over her heart. My name."

Her eyes were squeezed shut, tension written along her vibrating body. I took an unsteady step toward Red, prepared to do my best to knee him in the balls. Before I got the chance, Vinemont's iron grip encircled my upper arm and pushed me up onto the platform in the same rough fashion. He dropped me onto the table in front of the goblin and pushed me down until I lay prone.

The buzzing noise of the two other tattoo guns, mixed with poor Brianne's whimpers, reached my ears over the waves of music.

"What's it gonna be, Sin?"

The goblin knew Vinemont?

"The traditional V," Vinemont replied.

"Where?"

"Here." Vinemont's hand swiped the hair off my nape and let it hang down beside me in a curling cascade. He moved the emerald necklace up and out of the way. Then his cold finger traced a V on the back of my neck.

"Can do."

I had never gotten a tattoo. I'd thought about it plenty of times, but never had the conviction to get anything in particular. I used my body to make art. I didn't intend to be the art. And now, I was getting a tattoo forced on me. Nothing was my choice anymore. I'd signed it away.

For the millionth time since this ordeal started, I pictured my father. He was sitting by the fire in his favorite chair—safe, warm, no doubt sad, but alive. I would do what I had to do. I would cover my entire body in ink if it would save him.

Despite knowing this sacrifice was worth it, I wanted to go numb, to stop experiencing the horror of what was happening. I couldn't. I felt the cold table beneath me, felt the eyes of the masked people watching me as I was "branded," and I felt Vinemont standing next to me, no doubt enjoying my degradation moment by moment.

The goblin leaned down and whispered in my ear. "It's going to hurt, but I'll be as nice as I can."

"Thanks." *Did I just thank my torturer?*

The buzzing started close to my ear. I fisted my hands

as the first stinging pain erupted at the back of my neck.

"Good girl," the goblin said. "Just relax. I'm quick." Some more buzzing pain followed, punctuated by Red telling Brianne to shut her fucking mouth. "Well, at least all the girls say I'm quick."

Cruelty interspersed with sex jokes. This is what my life had become. I closed my eyes and let my arms fall, my knuckles brushing the floor as more pain ricocheted down my spine. I was an Acquisition, a possession to Vinemont. Nothing more. He would let the goblin mark my skin. He didn't care. He was still the cold spider I'd known him to be since the first time I saw him. I was in his web now, caught and dangling as he fed off me slowly. How would he win this competition? What would victory entail? My death?

I let the pain flow into me, trapping it inside a box in my heart. I'd store it up, feed it, make it grow stronger until it turned into rage. Then I would let it out and bring Vinemont and the rest of these accursed people to their knees.

CHAPTER TWELVE
SINCLAIR

SHE'D GONE LIMP. Given up. Tony continued his work, making a better V than even the one gracing my chest. He was my personal tattoo artist. His shop in Mobile was the toast of the South. People came from all over the country, all over the world, just to bear his ink.

He finished up the last of the thorns, done in the same deep green as mine, when I leaned down and added a little something extra.

"I want a small spider." I pointed to one of the inner curves of vines. "Here."

I whispered it low enough that Stella wouldn't hear it over the music and the buzzing. She always referred to me as a spider. Now, I would be on her body permanently.

"I like it, man." Tony switched to a deep crimson ink and drew in the small accent. "Nice."

One of the buzzing sounds stopped. Red's Acquisition sat up and yanked her dress back in place over her bare breast. I almost pitied her. That little show of skin was nothing compared to what came next.

I pitied her more for the garish tattoo Red had forced on her—his name in bright red ink with blue flames licking the letters. What a fucking prick to ruin a beautiful woman that way.

I shook my head. No, Red has his head in the game. Ruination was the goal. I was over here dicking around and ensuring Stella's brand was art, not something to mar her perfect skin. I'd told myself too many times to stop thinking of her as a person. But here I was, doing it again and letting my dick lead me around.

I'd already given in to her, promised her a reward for making it through this night. It was foolish. Still, if it worked even a little to keep her in line, it was worth it. This was spectacle, all of it. I needed the families, and especially Cal, to come away from this seeing me as the frontrunner for Sovereign.

Bob's Acquisition didn't fare much better than Red's. At least the eagle on his man's back had some artistry in it. It was nothing compared to Tony's work, but it turned out far better than the travesty on Brianne's chest.

"All right. She's all done." Tony sat back and admired his handiwork before rubbing some salve along Stella's skin.

It was a wasted effort. Her tattoo was the least of her worries.

Stella sat up and gave me the most vicious glare I'd ever seen on her face. Not even after the day in the yard had she flashed at me with such hate.

"Here, angel, check it in the mirror. It's not so bad."

Tony handed Stella a mirror and held one up behind her so she could see the design. Her crimson lips fell open. "That goddamn V? And what's the red thing. It looks like…" Her gaze shot up to my eyes. "A spider."

"Yes, indeed." Tony took her mirror and began packing up his tattoo gear.

"Head on out, Tony," I said. "Money's already in your account."

Tony popped his head up and surveyed the room. "Sure I can't stay and see if I can convince one of these masked freaky chicks to go home with me?"

Tony had no idea what was going on. I'd told him this was a fancy party with paid staff and entertainment, Stella and the other Acquisitions being the entertainment. He thought all this was voluntary and just a night of fun. If he stayed any longer, he would know just how non-consensual the whole thing was. I didn't want to alienate one of the true friends I actually had, and nothing alienates like slavery and whippings.

"No, man. No offense, but you don't have a chance with these women. Well, unless your bank account is bigger than I think."

"Definitely not. Okay, then. I'm out. Thanks again, Sin. And it was lovely working on you." He took Stella's hand and kissed it. "I'd love to see you in my shop sometime. Color you in some other areas."

She smiled at him. Actually smiled. "I'd like that."

Something roared to life inside me. It ripped at my ribs and tried to claw through my chest. Jealousy. Petty, overbearing, jealousy. I took her hand from his.

Tony laughed and jumped down from the platform. He gave a salute and then cut through the crowd and out one of the side doors.

"Why did you smile at him?" The ridiculousness of the question hit me only after I asked it.

"Because he was nice to me and he clearly had no idea what sort of fucked up shit you all are doing out here," She held my gaze, challenge in her bearing. "It's not his fault you dragged him into it."

"I didn't drag him into anything. I paid him well to create art on your body, and that's exactly what he did."

She raised her eyebrows and straightened her back. "You think the taint of this place doesn't rub off on people? You think he's unscathed?"

I grabbed her by the elbow. "He's a lot more unscathed than you're going to be."

"Fuck you."

Shit. Her anger shot straight to my cock, even in the middle of this crowd of devils. Her eyes flashed at me in unbridled fury.

"In time." I gave her the smile I knew she hated, the one that got under her skin.

She lifted a hand to strike me. I caught it and pulled it down, squeezing her wrist hard. "Do that again, and I'll hit back much, much harder. Understand?"

I wanted her to do it again, to knock my mask off so she could see the real me, the one who wanted to make it hurt, to fuck her, to make her scream. Her fear was easier for me to deal with than her anger. Her anger made me want to push her further, to take her to the edge, to make her beg me for something, anything. Her anger spurred me on to break her. Her fear let me know I was getting close.

The music piped down, the circling vultures slowing to a stop as Cal climbed atop the central platform again. "All right folks, brandings are done. Looks like we're ready for the big show."

Masked servants rushed in through the side doors with various pieces of equipment and furniture. Whips, chains, clamps, dildoes, spanking benches, couches, and too many beds to count. Once everything was in place, a cavalcade of prostitutes entered through the doors. Masked and nude, there was something for everyone—thin, ample, old, and young; they stood like low-hanging fruit, ready for the taking. The ballgoers flitted out and picked this one or that one, dragging the choice morsels back to their chosen spot of depravity.

I glanced down to Stella. She stood mesmerized. She'd unconsciously stepped closer to me as the hall geared up for the main event. Now, she was frozen in her horror, perhaps unable to comprehend the well of the evil in this room. It was deep, far too deep for anyone to plumb its depths. Especially not her. Naiveté swirled around her like a priceless perfume. The vein at her neck fluttered in a distressed rhythm. It was beautiful, like the pale wings of a butterfly—and just as fragile.

The orchestra kept playing softly as the dance floor became a sea of debauchery. Only a center strip was left open. The parade route.

"Come on, Acquisitions, don't be shy. Step on up. Time to really show us what you have to offer." Cal was gleeful.

I took Stella's hand and pulled her through the crowd, many of them already disrobing and setting on each other like wild animals. Fucking, biting, scratching. They left their masks on, as if it made any difference. The guest list was expertly curated. Any number of governors, wealthy socialites, business magnates, and others were congregated here tonight. The entire power structure south of the Mason Dixon was in this room, rutting like pigs and enjoying the show.

I dragged my sacrificial lamb behind me as she gasped at the spectacle all around her. Men and women clawed at her as she rushed past, their hunger bleeding over onto anyone and anything. Stella's purity was like a beacon. I sensed it, too. I wanted to drag her down and feast on her just like they did. But that wasn't what she was here for. Not yet.

We made it to the end of the cleared section of floor that bisected the entire hall and took our place behind Bob, Gavin, Red, and Brianne. The servants had quickly placed risers along the ground in a straight line so the walkway was elevated above the thriving mass of wickedness all around. Cries rose up and were drowned out by others. The orchestra continued playing as if nothing out of place were happening.

"Time to walk the walk, Acquisitions." Cal was crowing atop the podium as one of the prostitutes sucked his cock.

I hated the idea of him seeing Stella, of any of them seeing her. She was mine. But I kept having to share her.

Bob pushed Gavin up the stairs. "Walk."

Gavin obeyed, tentatively placing one foot in front of

the other. Once he'd made it a little way across, he was emboldened, holding his head a bit higher, his shoulders back. It made sense. After all, walking was easy.

He picked up his pace. When he got to the end of the walk, he turned to come back. Two men grabbed him, stripped off his coat, and then ripped his shirt away. He started to fight them but stopped when one held up a cattle prod. The other one pointed back down the runway.

Stella trembled next to me as Brianne broke down into gut-wrenching sobs. Red grabbed her by the hair and shook her. She screamed, high and piercing.

Stella reached out, fast as a cat, and gripped Red's arm, trying to wrest his grip from Brianne. Her small hands did nothing to stop him.

"Get your bitch under control, Vinemont, before I do it for you."

I wrapped my arm around Stella's waist and pulled her back. "Stop, Stella. You're making it worse."

She lunged at Red again as Brianne still suffered in his grasp. I held her back and away from him.

"What, you don't like this?" Red asked and shook Brianne again. He used his other hand and ripped down the back of her dress, leaving her top fully exposed. "What about this? Stella, is it? Do you like this?" Red ripped her dress again until the fabric fell to the floor.

"You, son of a bitch!" Stella cried.

"Oh, look over here. We have a wild one." Cal's voice grated on my ears as it boomed around the room.

I put my hand around Stella's throat and squeezed until she fell back against me gasping for air.

"Stop fighting," I hissed in her ear.

"Motherfucker. You, motherfuckers," was all she managed to get out.

Red sneered and stepped toward us.

"Back the fuck up, Red."

"Or what?"

"Or I'll stomp another mud hole in your ass, same as I

did at your sister's wedding last year. Remember that?"

"Fuck you, Sin."

"Right back at you, Red."

He returned to his toy, palming her ass so hard it had to hurt as she waited her turn. He leered at Stella as he did it, but she didn't make another move.

"You're all best friends, aren't you?" Stella's voice was quiet. "You're all the same. Let me go. I'll be *good*." She put an acid inflection on the last word.

Her comment should have stung me, but it was true. Red and I were the same breed. He was just playing the game better than I was at the moment. That would be remedied before the night ended.

I released Stella, but stayed ready to hold her again. I didn't know what Red would do if she actually managed to hurt him. It wouldn't be pretty. Not that I'd let him hurt her. That wasn't his right.

She stood in front of me, careful not to touch me. The back of her dress was open so I could see her smooth skin. She was so pale against the deep green of the dress. Flawless, radiant skin. I stared, knowing that it would never look this way again, not after tonight.

Gavin was on his final run, fully nude and halfway across the walkway back to us. Men and women rose from below to touch him. I froze at the thought of one of them touching Stella. But they would. There was nothing I could do to stop them.

"Go on, whore." Red pushed the shivering Brianne up onto the walkway. She wore only heels as she made her way between the revelers.

Many rushed to her, their fingers reaching to touch her pussy, her ass, her tits. Towards the middle, one man actually pulled her down and threw her on the nearest bed before trying to force her legs apart. Her scream blended with the others. Two servants approached and pulled the man off before setting her back on the platform. Now her shoes were missing and she was sobbing as she walked.

She made it to the other end and tried to stay there. It took a near miss with the cattle prod to get her moving again. By the time she made it back to us, her makeup was streaked from tears and her body shook with sobs.

"Again," Red demanded.

She shook her head. Red advanced on her with a menacing step.

"Go, just go. Get it over with." Stella urged the girl to pass through hell one more time. "You can do it. You have to."

Brianne focused on Stella who was nodding at her, encouraging her.

"I'll be here when you get back, okay? The faster you go, the faster it'll be done. And then it'll be my turn."

Red turned and put two fingers to his mouth in a 'V' before sticking out his tongue at Stella. "I can't wait."

I wanted to take out his knees, pound him into the ground, and then piss on his fucking corpse. Stella ignored him.

Brianne took the steps back up and made her final pass, far more quickly this time without heels. When she got back, Stella moved to embrace her but Red cut her off.

"Excellent work, whore. Maybe I'll only beat you once tonight." He turned to Stella. "Strip, bitch."

I hit him. I dropped him. I didn't even think. I just acted. Mistakes always seem to happen that way.

He rolled on the ground, hands to his face. He pushed his mask off and felt around his eye. "The fuck, Sin?"

Shit. This was not the plan. Getting angry and decking one of our number was definitely not part of a winning Acquisition.

Cal's laughing voice boomed over the sound system. "Now *that's* a show, ladies and gents!"

CHAPTER THIRTEEN
STELLA

RED PICKED HIMSELF up. He was shorter and smaller than Vinemont, but clearly angry. "You want to go outside?"

"No. But I may go over to your mother's place and release some aggression later." Vinemont smirked, clearly baiting Red.

Red swung. Vinemont backed out of the way easily and rushed forward, tackling Red to the ground. They devolved into a rolling, punching mass on the floor. I looked around. The nearest guests were focused on the fight. I took a few steps backwards, then a few steps more, then I was in the thick of the masked crowd. Some of them glanced at me and went back to their work. Others couldn't tear their attention away from the fight.

I turned and ran. I had no thought except escape. It was as if a host of klaxons were ringing in my head, my heart, alerting me to the mortal danger. I cut through the reaching hands and past the servants around the edges. I ran through the first open set of doors, my heels almost going out from under me as I turned the corner. I sped faster until a man stepped in front of me. I slammed into

111

his chest and he wrapped his arms around me.

"Going somewhere, Stella?"

I knew that voice. "Lucius?"

He dragged me sideways into an antechamber off the main hall and kicked the door closed behind us.

"The one and only." He held me close to him, his hands pressing into the bare skin at my back. A deep emerald mask hid his face, but I could see his eyes, light yet piercing. "Where were you going?"

"J-just away from there."

"Wouldn't that kill your father?" He slid a hand lower down my back.

Guilt crashed down on me. I had run from pure instinct, just as if I'd pulled my hand away from the fire. I couldn't do things like that. I had to leave my hand in the flames until it crisped and charred. My father's life depended on it.

"Yes."

"I could save you, you know?" His hand went lower, and slid beneath the fabric of my dress.

"What?"

"I mean, you'll still be an Acquisition for a year, nothing to be done about that. But you could choose me. You could tell Sin you'd rather be mine."

"You're even worse than he is." I tried to back away, but he held me fast and pinned me against his chest.

"Am I? Am I the one who threatened your father? Who prosecuted him? Who forced you into the contract?"

No. Vinemont had done all those things and more.

"See, Stella. I haven't hurt you or trapped you." His hand smoothed along my ass as he put his other hand at my chin and pulled my face up to his. "I could make this whole thing more bearable for you."

"I don't trust you." My voice was so breathy, like he'd taken the air from the room with his seductive words.

"You shouldn't." He leaned down, his lips so close to mine.

The door burst open as Vinemont crashed in. "Stella?"

"Another time, then?" Lucius whispered to me.

"What the fuck are you doing here?" Vinemont rushed to me, a trickle of blood flowing from his busted lip. "Get away from her."

Lucius released me. "I was just talking to her."

"Like hell you were." Anger rippled off Vinemont. "She's mine, Lucius. Leave her alone."

Vinemont stood behind me and wrapped a possessive hand around my neck. "Mine." It was more of a growl than a word.

Two servants rushed in behind Vinemont.

"I think you'll find this man doesn't have an invitation. You'll need to escort him out. Roughly."

"Come on, Sin." Lucius smiled.

Lucius's snake-like charm didn't work on Vinemont.

"Out."

Each servant grabbed one of Lucius' elbows and hustled him from the room.

"Later, Stella," he called. His voice echoed along the now-empty marble hallway.

Vinemont turned me around so I was forced to stare up into his unmasked face. "Did he hurt you?"

"Did *he* hurt me? Do you even hear yourself?"

Oakman strolled into the room. "Come on. Can't wait forever. The natives are getting restless for her walk and the rest of the festivities."

"Just another minute, Cal, if you don't mind." Vinemont didn't even turn to look at the host.

"That's all you'll get." The gameshow host tone drained from Cal's voice like water through a sieve. "Tradition can't be broken."

He shut the door behind him as he left.

"You can't run, Stella. I'll catch you. *They'll* catch you."

"The only one who caught me was Lucius."

"And you were lucky this time. You won't be so lucky again. Trust me."

This was such a mindfuck. He acted like he cared one way or another what happened, but I knew all he cared about was winning this twisted competition. He wasn't fooling me. No one was. Fuck him. Fuck all of them. I stepped away from him and walked to the door.

"Where are you going?"

"To do my walk of shame. Are you going to help me out of this dress or what?"

I'd never seen shock on his face. If he weren't a monster, it would have been almost cute. He followed me back into the ballroom, new debauches going on all around as the ballgoers got their second wind. I didn't see the other Acquisitions.

Once lined up at the walkway, I reached behind me to unhook my dress. Then I realized I had no idea how Enid had put the thing on me.

Vinemont was at my back then, his fingers pulling the fabric together and unhooking the closures that must have held it together along the center seam. He moved his hands up to my shoulders and inhaled deeply before slipping his fingers beneath the lace straps and letting the dress fall to the floor in a feathery heap.

Cold air rushed over my body, and the nearest revelers stopped what they were doing to watch me.

Vinemont moved his hands down my sides, feeling my curves before his hands settled at my hips. His breath was warm against my shoulder. His familiar scent was oddly comforting.

I took one step, and then another. I kept my head high as I walked. I fixed my gaze far across the room on one of the particularly beautiful chandeliers. Crystal drops hung from it, multi-faceted and shimmering despite the mass of human ugliness beneath it. It was untouched by the hideous inhabitants of the room. Maybe I could be, too.

I slapped away hands and fingers, refusing to let them degrade me any more than they already had. I ignored catcalls and whistles. When I reached the end, I turned and repeated my travel, glaring at Oakman as defiantly as I could. He stared back intently before unzipping his fly and motioning for one of the women below to "assist" him.

I dropped my attention and caught Vinemont staring at me, fire in his eyes like never before. He didn't look down my body, just held my gaze as I walked, as if he were pulling me toward him with some strange gravity. I reached him and turned, making the circuit one more time under the watchful eyes and the grasping hands.

I reached the far end where a wrinkled man with a protruding erection waited for me.

"Ms. Rousseau, so pleased to see you again." He grinned, a red mask obscuring his eyes, while his date for the night—a handsome man of no more than twenty—stood close behind him.

I knew his voice. My stomach flipped and soured. "Judge Montagnet?"

The judge's date reached around and began stroking Montagnet's cock, though the set of the young man's mouth was less excited and more apathetic.

"Well, I must get back," Montagnet said. "I just wanted to congratulate you. Keep up the good work, lovely girl, and I certainly hope the Vinemonts prevail this year. Don't worry. I'll keep an eye on your father for you." He disentangled himself from the younger man's grip and knelt down on all fours on a nearby divan. I turned my head away before I saw anything more.

The judge's threat was a strangling vine around my heart, choking out any love or warmth, leaving only cold fear. I was foolish, so foolish for running. Never again. I was captured, bound by the invisible vise of these people, their power. There was nowhere to run, nowhere to turn. I scanned the crowd, wishing I could burn the chateau down on their heads.

One of the servants motioned toward me with the prod. I took a deep breath and finished my walk. I kept my eyes up, trying to distance myself from the horror of the scene. I refused to give in to the helpless feeling of being nude and on display for the faceless horde. They thrashed around me like damned souls in hell, their breaths hot and their hands clawing at me. I fought them off and hurried my pace.

No one managed more than a brushing swipe against my bare skin. I counted it as a win. Vinemont's gaze was still rapt, though every so often he would stare daggers at the ones who reached out to touch me.

When I made it back to him, he offered his hand to me as I stepped down. I didn't take it.

"Well, now that we've got the easy parts over with, let's get on to the main attraction!" Oakman, as ever, kept the entertainment fresh.

I glared up at Vinemont. "Wait, *that* wasn't the main attraction?"

He showed no emotion, just held my gaze. He was somehow steady even as I felt the storm rising around me.

"Bring them on up," the voice boomed.

Vinemont squeezed my arm and pushed me in front of him, toward the stairs and to the tree. Gavin and Brianne were ahead of me. As they made it to the top, I heard metallic clanging sounds above. Brianne shrieked.

"We haven't even hurt you yet." Oakman's laughter infected the room until it was a cacophony of soulless mirth.

I took the final step. Brianne was sobbing again. Gavin just looked catatonic, as if none of this was registering any more. They were both chained, their fronts facing the tree. Vinemont guided me to the one empty spot against the trunk. He raised my wrists and clamped the shackles down around each one. He pulled the chain down from above and hooked it to the chain in the center of the restraints. Then he fastened my ankles with the restraints at the base of the tree.

I shook. I couldn't stop it. I couldn't stay strong in the face of what I knew was coming. Oakman stood and trailed the end of a whip through his hand lovingly. Moving slowly, I bet the leather was smooth and supple. Moving as he swung, it would tear my flesh. My tremor grew until the shackles were shaking, clanging against each other.

"Oh, I can fix that." Oakman yanked on a chain hanging from a pulley next to him. It pulled our arms upward until all three of us were pressed against the tree, the metal digging into our wrists and ankles and our backs on display.

"Everyone, the years just keep getting better don't they?"

A smattering of approval rose from below. Even with the spotlight in my face, I could sense they were all still, watching. A tremor roared through me at the realization. What could be so fascinating to stop the roiling beasts from clamoring and rutting?

I tried to turn, to look at Vinemont. To try and will him to free me, save me, let me go. I couldn't see him. The blinding light and tight bonds mastered me. I was held fast, blood already running down my forearms from the shackles. The pain in my wrists and ankles was growing by the second, the metal cutting deeper with each of my breaths.

"Two-hundred and fifty years of pride. And this year is the best of all. Twenty-five Acquisition Balls, twenty-five strokes of the whip for each of our guests."

The crowd roared with approval.

I couldn't stop the sob that rattled up from my lungs. Brianne began screaming, her voice a high, blood-curdling shriek. It died away, muffled by Red's handkerchief or some similar gag.

My thoughts scattered, unable to focus on anything. I clamped my eyes shut and forced myself to focus on why I was here. Dad. He was there on the back of my eyelids. Standing over me as I awoke in the hospital. He smoothed my hair from my face even as I was bandaged and strapped to the bed. Was this so different? I bled, I was bound, I was wavering between the world I'd known and one I could only imagine. But now, instead of breaking him, my suffering would save him. Tears slid down my cheeks and disappeared. I would endure it. All of it.

"Now, who wants to go first?" Cal broke through my memories.

"That'd be me." Vinemont spoke, his voice harsh and strong.

"That's my good man. Here you go. Make them count." Oakman laughed.

Vinemont stood behind me and ran a lingering hand down my skin, the whip hanging from his other hand. His touch was warm, somehow gentle. I let myself feel it, if only for a second. Let myself imagine he cared for me, that his was a lover's touch. That he wouldn't hurt me.

The warmth disappeared. He backed away.

I held my breath. I felt like the entire room held its breath. And then I was awash in pain. I didn't know I'd screamed until the sound died in my lungs from the force of the next hit.

"He's really going all out. This may be your next Sovereign ladies and—"

I couldn't hear his words, couldn't hear anything except the sound of my pain. It was my scream, eating up the space inside me, bleeding out my ears. Agony like I had never felt before erupted along my back. Lines of destruction. I could feel my skin separating with each of his vicious strokes. Blood leaked and trailed down my legs. It felt the same as I remembered it from those years ago, the same way as my blood felt dripping from my arms. But this time the damage was bigger and offered no promise of release from this life.

I screamed until my voice left me, the air no longer cooperating with my lungs. I burned everywhere. My blood sprayed against Brianne whose stifled scream replaced my own.

I couldn't breathe. I couldn't see. I was gone.

CHAPTER FOURTEEN
STELLA

MY MOM STROKED her warm hand down my face. Even in the dark I knew it was her. She whispered comforting words to me, telling me the pain was temporary and would fade. The sharp stings were far away now. Everything beneath me was soft, warm. I was loved. I was content.

My back was cool, numb. What happened?

I tried to tell her how much I missed her, how glad I was she was back. She'd been gone so long. Where had she gone?

"Shh, sleep now." Mom pulled a blanket up to my waist, making my legs toasty.

"Go ahead and push more before she feels anything." She was speaking to someone else now.

Deep dreamless sleep.

The sound of birds pulled me up from the pleasant darkness. Light streamed in through the windows of the room. I faintly recognized the walls, the windows, the quilts, all jogging my memories. I was lying on my stomach.

I blinked the sleep away and lifted my head. An aching pain shot through my back. I dropped my head back down with a groan.

"Stella." It was my mother's voice. No. No, it was Renee's. Mom was dead.

"Renee?" I could barely speak, my voice hoarse.

Is there a tube in my arm?

"I'm here. Don't worry. You're healing up nicely. Do you want to go back under again?"

"Under?"

"Asleep. The Vinemont family doctor has been staying for the past three days and keeping you asleep so you could recover. I can have him put you out for longer if it bothers you too much."

My mind was having trouble clicking into the 'on' position. An IV was suspended above me, some clear liquid dripping through it at a leisurely pace.

I shifted my head so I could see Renee. Her concerned face brought the flood of horror back. The ball, the tortures, Vinemont flaying the skin from my back.

A sob rose up and stuck in my dry throat.

Renee wrung her hands. "I'll fetch Dr. Yarbrough."

"No," I croaked.

I fought the tears back, though a few escaped and dropped onto my white pillow. We were silent for a long time. The ball replayed through my mind like a particularly vivid nightmare—the masks, the cruelty, the violence, and the pain. More than anything, I remembered Vinemont, how he'd volunteered to whip me first, how he'd swung harder and harder until I blacked out from the pain.

Had I actually almost felt something for him? Each lash killed whatever twisted emotion had grown in my heart. I was glad. My feeling of betrayal was replaced with rage, raw anger. I added these to the box in my chest, the one where I had hidden away my sadness. It was full to bursting with every negative emotion I possessed. Still, I stuffed more inside, poisoning myself by saving the bitterness and hate.

I tried to calm my breathing. Anytime my lungs expanded too fully, my back felt as if it would rip apart. Renee looked almost as white as my pillowcase and kept wringing her hands.

"Vinemont?"

"I haven't seen him. Not since he brought you back. He was, well, he was in a bad way. Lucius and Teddy had to come get him."

"Tired out from whipping me, was he?"

"No, not that. It did something to him. I don't know."

"Did something to *him*, huh?" I tried to yell, but it only came out in a hoarse burst of sound. The effort made my back scream.

"I meant. I-I meant—" She rose abruptly and came to take my hand.

I wanted to rip it away, but I didn't dare move.

"I mean, I've never seen him like that. He kept begging me to fix it, to heal you. He tried to clean your wounds himself before Dr. Yarbrough arrived. He wouldn't let anyone else touch you. He sat here with you and told you he was sorry over and over. He wouldn't leave. Not until Lucius and Teddy came. Only Teddy could get through to him. I haven't seen Mr. Sinclair since."

I couldn't imagine any of what she was saying. Remorse seemed a completely foreign emotion to Vinemont. The way he'd whipped me was an assault on more than just my body. He'd struck at my soul, instilling dread so deeply that I didn't know if I'd ever recover.

When I'd hurt myself, it gave me a release, a chance at oblivion. When he'd done it, he trapped me even more inside myself. Every lash was a fresh set of bars, hemming me in and holding me captive. If he could do that to me, what else would he be willing to do to win the Acquisition? And what was even required to win?

"I know it's hard. I know." Renee's voice broke through my shadowy thoughts.

"You know? No, you don't." I slid my fingers away from her, out of her warm grip.

She knelt by my bed, getting at eye level with me.

"I do, Stella."

No you don't.

"How? Have you been branded and whipped? Have you had a year of your life stolen? Have you had to endure a man like Vinemont?" My tears were flowing, making slight plops onto the pillow beneath me.

Renee's dark eyes were troubled, a storm seeming to rage in her breast. She took a deep breath, as if she had come to a decision. She began unbuttoning her black shirt, her fingers nimble. Then she turned and swept her hair away from her nape. There in the stark green and black was the same 'V' that had been seared into me in ink.

She pulled her top down further so I could see the beginnings of lash marks crisscrossing her fair skin.

"What—"

"I was Mrs. Sinclair's Acquisition twenty years ago." She faced me again, her frank gaze disarming me.

If she had hit me, I couldn't have been more stunned. A million questions tumbled through my mind, one building on the next before stumbling in front of an even bigger curiosity. Why would she stay? What had her year been like? Could she help me?

She stood and refastened her top. When she moved to step away from me, I reached for her. The pain shot like lightning down my back. It went so deep I wondered if my heart hadn't somehow been lashed right along with my skin. I screamed and dropped my head.

"I'll get the doctor. Don't move, sweet Stella. Please don't." She rushed from the room.

My mind spun with revelations and harsh sensations. Renee had known all along. She knew what would happen to me at the ball. Why didn't she warn me? Vinemont's words came back to me—the more I knew, the more afraid I would be, and the more it all would hurt.

A dark figure rushed through the door, Renee sweeping in behind. Before I could protest—did I want to protest?—he fiddled with my IV and I was out.

This time I dreamed. Vinemont was in there in all of them—tormenting me or loving me. Were they one and the same? Then my father was sitting in his favorite chair telling me a story, though I couldn't hear the words. Finally, my mother arrived, her hair up in the messy bun I remembered. She was sad. Always sad. Water flowed from her mouth and then it changed to blood, more blood than a person could lose and still live. She was drowning in the very thing that gave her life. I couldn't save her. I couldn't even save myself. I sat in a pool of my own blood, the droplets slowing right along with my heartbeat. Steps in the hallway—my father. I dreaded him finding me before it was over. I didn't want him to see me die. The footsteps grew louder and then stopped.

"Stella?"

I knew that voice. It wasn't my father's. It was the voice of a demon, one that made me burn with desire and hate until both emotions mixed in a funeral pyre of black smoke.

I opened my eyes. He was here. Vinemont.

"Going to hit me again?" It came out as a whisper, but he winced as if I'd yelled at him.

"I don't know."

I was still lying on my stomach. My eyes finally adjusted to the dark. He sat near the door, his face unshaven, his clothes wrinkled and disheveled. He looked like I felt.

"What sort of an answer is that?"

"An honest one." He leaned over, resting his elbows on his thighs.

"You sick fuck." I refused to cry. *I would not cry.*

"Yes." He scrubbed a hand over his face. The sound of his palm rubbing against his stubble was loud in my ears.

"What now? Are you going to hurt me some more? Maybe cut some fingers off and send them to my dad? Fuck you. Whatever it is, just get it over with." Tiredness had settled into every muscle and bone of my body. It must have been the drugs. My back no longer felt so raw; only a low ache emanated from it. My skin felt as if it had stitched back together, but I could already sense the scars forming, solidifying, forever marking me.

"No, I would never..."

I laughed but it was a rough, ugly sound. "You would *never?* Never what? Never enslave me? Never strip me naked and make me bleed for an audience?" My eyes welled with unshed tears. The hurt inside me seemed too much for my body to bear.

He dropped his head, his defeat just as out of character as his unshaven face and mussed hair. "I can't change what I did, Stella. I would do it again."

I wanted to scream, to rage at him, to demand to know why he sat here appearing contrite, while at the same time telling me he would do it all over again if given the chance. Was this the mental torture to go along with the physical?

"Do me a favor. When you become Sovereign, how about you make your first decree for you to go royally fuck yourself?"

He sighed and shook his head. "I don't expect you to understand. I didn't want—"

"Get out." I turned my head away from him, my neck stiff and unused to the movement.

He stayed. I could sense him there, unmoving, his gaze still on me.

There was nothing more to say. He'd whipped me like an animal. Worse, really. The memory of Cal Oakman's voice rattled around in my mind. The way he crowed over Vinemont's fevered strokes that drew my blood so easily.

My tears went from sadness to rage.

I was a furious tempest of hatred and loathing but I was trapped in my battered body. All I could do was wish my tears away and accept that Vinemont had damned me to this existence. This life of pain and hurt and darkness. So many shadows that I never even knew existed had eclipsed any faint light I may have once had. I had been snuffed out, destroyed by the man who now looked so lost.

After a long moment, the floor creaked, and I heard his retreating footsteps.

"Wait," I said.

He returned with a quicker step, standing behind me now.

"You said I could have a reward if I got through the ball."

"Yes." His voice crackled, almost hopeful.

"I want to see my father and stepbrother."

He shifted and another long silence fell like deep winter snow, muffling and burying us. He touched the edge of my bed, the hesitant movement making me angry, making me want to hurt him.

"Okay." He sighed, resignation in the rush of air.

"You're going to keep your word?"

He ghosted his fingers through my hair. I closed my eyes, wondering if he had any chance of calming the firestorm that raged in my breast.

"I always do." His voice was as soft as his caress.

I wanted to believe this was truly who he was—the man who seemed just as wrecked by what he'd done as my tattered flesh. But which one of him was real? The destroyer or the destroyed? Either way, my tears still fell, my pain still stung, my heart still ached. He had done this and would do it again. I pushed any tender thoughts away.

"I want to see them soon. But not until I'm healed all the way. Or at least as much as I can heal from what you did. I don't want them to see me like this."

"You just tell me when and I'll arrange it." He gave my hair one last gentle stroke. He hesitated. Words were on his lips. I could sense them lingering there in the dark. Instead of voicing them, he turned and strode out, his pace clipped.

I was left alone with my pain, all the varying shades of it. I turned my head back to look at the chair where he'd sat. My gaze roamed further up and seized on the discordant quilt created by Vinemont's mother. What sort of person made it through the Acquisition and won?

I heard more steps, and recognized them as Renee's. She slowed to a quiet tiptoe by the time she reached my door. Her black skirt rustled softly as she sat and folded her hands in front of her.

"I want to get up."

She rose and smoothed my hair over my shoulder. "Sunrise is in an hour. Rest until then."

Comfort was in her movements, her touch. I didn't want comfort. I wanted to stop crumbling, to shore up what pieces of me I had left.

"No, I'm done resting. Help me sit up or I'll do it by myself."

I couldn't lie in bed for another minute. I couldn't stand being helpless and weak. I wouldn't be. Not anymore.

With Renee's help, I recovered over the next few weeks. I didn't see Vinemont or Lucius at all during that time. I would pass Teddy in the hallway sometimes. He would smile and exchange pleasantries. Underneath, I could sense he was troubled. I had too many problems of my own to even begin to care about his. He seemed like a nice guy, but he was born into a pit of vipers. It would be foolish to think he wouldn't bite just as surely as Vinemont and Lucius did.

I began to realize he was the only one who knew less than I did about what was going on. Renee wouldn't tell me anything new, only that Vinemont didn't volunteer for the Acquisition. It was done on some sort of lottery basis.

I'd figured as much at the ball when the names of the families were called. Oakman made it seem as if it were some "luck of the draw" situation, though it seemed like a stroke of bad fortune to be chosen. Even so, I couldn't forgive Vinemont. He didn't have to choose *me*. He didn't have to threaten my father and force me into the contract. I didn't wish this on another soul, but I couldn't excuse his turning a bad stroke of luck on his part into a year-long suffering on mine.

"I honestly still don't know how they're picked," she said one day over a steaming mug of tea after I'd pestered her for the better part of an hour.

The weather had finally turned cooler, leaves swirling in the yard and the grass fading into a dormant brown. I preferred hot chocolate, and stirred the marshmallows around in the foam before taking a scorching sip.

"Well, tell me something, anything. What's next? Is there something next?" I hoped there wasn't. I hoped it would be just a year of captivity spent here with her. I wasn't a total idiot, though. I knew that little fairy tale was too good to be true.

She set the mug down and stared into the rolling steam. "I'll tell you this and no more. There are more trials. The next one is at Christmas."

I raised an eyebrow at the all-around fucked up quality of holiday-based tortures.

"And then there's another in the spring, and the final one in the summer. I won't give details."

After that revelation, she was close-lipped, and always answered my questions with a deflection or a suggestion that I get it directly from the source—Vinemont. No matter how many times she reiterated the fact that Vinemont didn't choose to participate in the Acquisition, I couldn't forget the verve with which he pursued the Sovereign title, the way he'd played to the audience of masked ghouls. I still didn't know what it would take for him to win, but if the exhibition of my body and the whipping were any indication, it wouldn't be a pleasant outcome for me. So, no, I wouldn't speak to him.

Despite her stonewalling on the Acquisition process, Renee and I fell into a happy pretend friendship, as if we didn't share a dark secret of slavery and sadism. She was more than happy to discuss just about any subject I could think of other than the one I was desperate to learn about. We'd spend time in the house's library, reading quietly as the days faded. No one ever stopped us from exploring, and Renee showed me the ins and outs of the kitchen wing, the guest wing, and several other areas that had rooms upon rooms full of remarkable possessions and ornate furniture. Farns was always happy to see us, and gave us the history of various antiques and treasures scattered around the common rooms.

We even stopped in Vinemont's room once. It had his scent, masculine and clean. It drew me. I wanted to know more about him, to pick him apart in an effort to find out how he ticked so maybe I could somehow gum up the mechanism.

His room was modest, more modern and Spartan than the rest of the house. A king size bed with white duvet, navy walls, and minimal furniture filled the large space. No photos of him or his family graced the walls. I wandered to his nightstand when Renee wasn't looking and pulled the top drawer open.

Instead of skin mags or back issues of "Psychotic Monthly," there was nothing except for a single black feather. I recognized it immediately. It had come from the dress I'd worn to the ball. It mocked me, reminiscent of the forsaken glass slipper. Except Vinemont was no prince. He was the devil.

I slammed the drawer shut.

Lucius' room was more colorful, white walls covered with tons of art—much of it good, to my surprise. He was messier than Vinemont. Books and magazines were scattered across his desk. There was an iPod and earbuds that somehow managed to make their way into my pocket.

"Where are they anyway?"

"Mr. Sinclair is in town for work, I believe. Mr. Lucius is in South America visiting two of the sugar cane plantations. He's in charge of the business while Mr. Sinclair handles the legal issues and keeps up appearances as parish district attorney. He never wanted the position, but the Sovereign decreed that Mr. Sinclair would take the post, and that was that."

"I thought the parish district attorney was elected?"

Renee raised a cynical black eyebrow. "And I thought slavery was illegal."

"Touché. What about Teddy?"

"He's in school still, in Baton Rouge. I'm not sure what he intends to do. It's not as if he has too many options."

"How does a rich, handsome young man like Teddy not have many options?"

"Depends on what the Sovereign says. If Oakman decides Teddy should be a lawyer, then off to law school he goes. If he decides being a doctor would be better, then med school."

"The Sovereign wields that much power?"

"More than you can even imagine. Who do you think decides the winning Acquisition? And it's worse for the Vinemonts, really. Even though they've been part of the ruling faction for well over a hundred and fifty years, some families still remember that it wasn't always so. The others try and lord it over them. The Vinemonts used to be poor sharecroppers and seamstresses. Worked for the Oakmans for years and years until..." Renee put her hand to her mouth as if that would somehow stop her words from spilling out.

"What? Until what?" I didn't want her to stop. All this was news to me and I was starved for information.

"Oh, nothing. I shouldn't have said. It's all ancient history. It's just, those things aren't really talked about. Not in the house, especially."

"If it's ancient history, then why can't you talk about it? What harm could there be?"

"Mr. Lucius should be home in a couple of days." I'd learned that Renee's subject change signaled the end of the conversation, despite my many unsuccessful attempts to make it otherwise.

There was only one part of the house we never visited—the top floor.

"It's mostly shut off and dusty. No one goes up there, really. Not anymore." Renee always led me away from the stairs to the third floor, even when I had placed a foot hesitantly on the bottom step. The steps weren't dusty, and I got the feeling Renee's hurried explanation was hiding something more. Then again, this house was full of secrets—Renee's not the least among them.

A few days later Renee and I were whiling away the afternoon in the library. I still hadn't set eyes on Lucius or Vinemont since my recovery. I sometimes caught myself wondering what Vinemont was doing, where he was. Then I reminded myself of the scars on my back and turned my thoughts elsewhere.

Renee sat under a throw blanket and read as I tried to paint. She had ordered every supply I could think of to get my art started again. But for the third day in a row, I just stared at the blank canvas.

Before, I would let whatever I was feeling meld itself to the canvas. Now, it was as if my emotions were in too much of a vicious muddle to do anything other than a Picasso imitation, my pieces scattered in ways that reflected how fragmented I was inside.

My back had healed. It no longer stung or ached, but I

knew it was different, scarred. Renee smeared some sort of specialty cream she'd ordered from Juliet over my back every night. She said my scars had already faded much more than her own. Even then, she wouldn't tell me about her Acquisition, about why she lingered here in this house.

While I was lost in my thoughts, my hands worked on the canvas of their own accord. Before I knew it, I'd drawn out a harsh line, then another, then another. I worked feverishly, sketching a body drawn impossibly tight and covered with the crisscrossing lines. I drew and shaded until the image came forth from the white background just as it had done in my mind.

The canvas was macabre even without color. The woman's head lolled to the side. A hand with a whip reared back as if the aggressor stood where I did, on this side of the easel, ready to inflict more violence. When I finally changed to paint, mixing the colors with a rough hand, I realized it had grown late. Renee slept on the couch, a book resting against her softly rising and falling chest.

I woke her gently and sent her on to bed before returning to my work, intent on finishing what I'd begun. I smoothed on the crimson, letting the painting run in streaky rivers before sweeping through them with the edge of my brush. I let that part dry and worked on the edges and background. I swiped my hand on my long skirt, leaving a streak that I knew would never come out.

Vines in blacks and greens—matted, twisting, and snakelike—grew from my brush strokes. They looked as venomous as I'd intended, threatening from the canvas, seeking to taste the crimson of the foreground. They wrapped around the nude woman's ankles and wrists.

When I finished, I stepped away, giving a critical eye to the piece. It was dark and needed a good deal of touching up, but it was my soul in pencil and paint. The darkness infecting me had leached onto the bristles and then the threads. Would getting it out keep the rot from going any deeper?

"You captured it."

I whirled. Vinemont stood behind me, so close that I didn't know how I hadn't heard him. He was clean shaven again, well put together. He wore a suit, the tie loosened and his top button undone. His eyes, though, were haunted. They were still his deep, turbulent blue. Beneath them were gray circles, unease or worry having left its mark.

"You look well," he said.

"Do I?" I crossed my arms over my chest, not caring that I got paint all over my shirt. It wasn't the first time. "Maybe you should see my back. It might change your mind."

He finished the job on his tie, pulling it loose so it hung open around his neck. "I did what I had to do, Stella."

A burning rage erupted in my chest, my mind. My anger had simmered for so long that seeing his face forced it to boil over. But what made it worse, what really sent me over the edge, was that some part of me recognized a change in him. The things he'd said to me that night in my room, the way he looked now—none of it fit with what he'd said about willingly hurting me again.

"Why?" I met his gaze.

"Because you're my Acquisition. Because I have to win."

"So you'd do anything it takes to win, to be Sovereign?"

"To win? Yes." His face hardened, becoming the cruel mask I knew so well. "I will do everything in my power to win."

"Then why are you here? Why even come speak to me until it's time for my yuletide whipping?"

"Renee told you?" He shook his head and anger flashed in his tired eyes.

"Yes. She told me I have a very busy holiday schedule over the next few months."

"What else did she tell you?"

"Nothing. You've got her well trained."

He ran a hand through his dark hair. "Not me."

"Then who?"

He took a step toward me. I matched it, stepping backward.

A shadow crossed his face—pain? Then it was gone and he fisted his hands at his sides, hell in his eyes.

"Look, Stella, this is something that neither of us can avoid. I'm doing what I have to do. That's all you need to know about it. Once your year is up, you can leave and never look back. Until that time, I need you to do as I ask and just accept it. No more questions. No more trying to run."

"I'm not running."

"Keep it that way." He took another step toward me, menacing.

I held my ground. He could hurt me, but I wouldn't give him the benefit of my fear. I stared into him, past the blue and deeper, watching as they turned from anger to heat. The air in the room shifted, like an electrical current hummed between us.

All the concern that he'd walked in with was gone. He looked...hungry, as if the moon had emerged from behind a cloud and revealed him to be some sort of ravenous wolf.

His gaze travelled my face, my body. When heat erupted along my skin as if he'd touched me, I knew I was damned. To want the touch of the devil was nothing short of a mortal sin.

I struck him, my open palm whipping across his face with a satisfying slap. He didn't retaliate, just tilted his head to the side until his neck popped in the most unnerving fashion. What had been fire in his eyes was now a raging inferno.

He advanced, only inches from me now. I pulled my hand back to strike him again, but he caught it, squeezing my wrist painfully. I tilted my chin up, meeting his vicious encroachment with defiance. He wouldn't frighten me out of this space. It was mine. I didn't care if the entire place was covered in fucking vines, I would slash and burn them until I'd cleared an area for me, my paint, my books, and my own bit of freedom.

Quick as an adder, he put his free hand to my face. I didn't flinch, though I expected him to strike me. The heat in his gaze spoke of something explosive—violence or desire, maybe a heady mix of both. When his palm touched my skin, my eyes closed involuntarily.

"So soft." His voice was tinged with wonder.

I was down the rabbit hole, everything topsy-turvy and wrong, because his touch—god, his touch. It was like I'd been starving for it this entire time but didn't know it. When I opened my eyes, he leaned down, his lips teasing mine with the bare millimeters of distance. He was a gorgeous villain, a predator dressed up as a man.

I raised my unrestrained hand to hit him again, but he caught it, too, and wrenched both of them behind my back. He pressed me into his chest, caging me with his body. I could feel the blaze emanating from him, the desire like a heat wave. Could he feel mine? His gaze held me fast, furious and possessive. He looked at me like I was *his*. Not because of a contract, not because of the Acquisition, but because the intensity of his desire made it so. He would have what he wanted. His gaze flicked down to my mouth and he dipped his head lower, his breath grazing my lips.

I burned to destroy him, to leave him in flames as I walked away from the ashes. But first ... just a kiss. I pushed up on my tip toes.

Our lips met.

I was lost.

He wasn't gentle. I knew he wouldn't be. I still wanted him. His lips were soft and firm, taking everything and demanding more. His tongue probed against my lips.

When he pulled my hair back, I arched into him and opened my mouth. His tongue was a wicked explorer, caressing mine and tasting me in a way no one ever had.

He groaned and wrapped an arm around me, crushing me against him. His scent was in my nose, floating in my lungs like a whirlwind, putting me even further under his spell. My nipples rubbed against him, the tips hard and wanting. They ached for his touch, his mouth. I had never known the sheer need that welled up inside me, the wetness between my thighs, the desperate feeling of wanting more and still more.

He lifted me and carried me to the sofa, laying me down and looking over his prize. He yanked off his blazer and pulled his shirt away, buttons flying as his hard abs were revealed. The same V as mine was inked over his heart, the intricate vines spreading and roping along his chest and down his arms.

I licked my lips, and his gaze went straight to the movement. He was the spider I'd always imagined him to be, lethal and beautiful.

He stalked on top of me, wedging himself between my thighs. His hands were at the hem of my shirt, pushing it up and peeling it off my body. He hitched in a breath when he saw I wasn't wearing a bra.

"Fuck, Stella," he rasped.

He pressed a hard kiss on each nipple. My stomach tightened and clenched.

I dug my fingers through his hair, scratching him as he took a nipple in his mouth. I arched my back off the sofa. His mouth was hot as he teased the hard tip. He circled his tongue around the pearled peak before pulling it in his mouth against his teeth. The sensation went straight to my pussy, making it pulse with want. When he sucked my nipple hard enough to bruise, I couldn't stifle my cry. He was going to devour me, just like his eyes had always promised.

He relinquished my breast to move up and reclaim my

mouth. His hard length rested against my pussy. It promised more pleasure than I'd ever felt. I dug my nails into his shoulders, wanting to hurt him, to mark him just as he'd done to me. I bit his lip, drawing blood. He groaned and kissed me roughly, making me taste his copper on my tongue. I was on fire, rage and hatred mixing with the most primal need. I wanted him bleeding, but I also wanted him buried deep inside me. I wanted him screaming in pain but also in the most resplendent pleasure.

As our mouths warred, blood welled around my nails where I broke his skin. He rocked his hips against me, making my clit buzz with the power of his stroke. He gripped my hair, pulling until I cried out. When I opened my mouth, he sank his tongue inside me, claiming me. I gave in. I opened for him, letting him taste me, letting him own me. He kissed me so ferociously that my breath was gone and I was breathing only him.

He slid a hand down to my neglected breast and palmed it as he rubbed a thumb over my nipple. I moaned into his mouth, his tongue swirling the sound around before he swallowed it. He was possessing me, branding me far more than any ink on my neck or any scars on my back. His touch, his insistent kiss marked me deeper, surer than any lash ever could. I was betraying myself. I knew it. I didn't care. I didn't want anything other than him, his hands, his body, his kiss. I had never felt more alive.

He pushed a hand between us, yanking my skirt up before roughly pulling my panties to the side. When he touched my wet core, he groaned. I wanted him inside me. I wanted him wild, desperate. I wanted him to come for me, only me.

"You are so wet," he grated. He released my breast and gripped my hair, yanking my head to the side and sucking on the tender skin of my neck.

His fingers strummed me, playing me until I writhed beneath him. Wanton and desperate for his touch. He was the most delicious thing I had ever felt.

"You like that, Stella?" he murmured against me.

"Yes," I breathed.

"How about this?" He sank a finger inside.

I gasped, the breath hitching in my throat at the unbridled pleasure. He withdrew it and pushed it in again. My hips ground up into him.

"Fucking my finger, Stella? Just wait until it's my cock, filling every last bit of your tight cunt."

I thought I might come just from his words. No one had ever spoken to me that way. I needed more.

He sat back on his haunches. "Don't move." A growl to match the animal look on his face.

He pushed my skirt up past my hips. With one hand, he ripped my panties away. Then he fixed his gaze on my pussy. I was bare to him, completely open and at his mercy in a way I'd never been, not even when I was chained and whipped. This was the most intimate moment I'd ever had.

"I can't stop." He slowly brought his gaze to mine. "I won't."

I swallowed hard, his taste still on my lips. "Don't."

CHAPTER FIFTEEN
SINCLAIR

IT TOOK EVERY remaining shred of self-control I had not to rip my fly open and shove into her. Her glistening pink flesh was something I'd fantasized about and now…to have it laid out before me like an offering was almost too much.

I drew down my zipper and pulled my cock from my boxers. It throbbed in my palm. I didn't want my skin. I wanted hers. Every inch of it.

Her eyes grew wide as she saw my cock, hard and ready for her. I slid my tip against her slick folds and almost lost my seed all over her. I gripped up on the base, keeping myself in check.

She scooted back from me. Not happening. I dragged her back down beneath me and caged her throat with my hand.

"It's too big, Sinclair. I-I don't think I can."

She said my name. I always wanted her to call me Sinclair, though she insisted on Vinemont. The former was a surrender, the latter a curse. All I needed from her right now was total surrender, submission. I would have it.

"I haven't done this since Dylan and I—"

I silenced her by forcing two fingers inside. She moaned and closed her eyes. I didn't want to hear about anyone else touching what was mine. After tonight, they would be erased. I would fuck her so completely that I was her first, her last, her everything. My cum on her—in her—would mark her as mine.

Still holding her fast with one hand, I stroked her clit with my fingertips. The fear drained from her as I worked her into a frenzy. Her clit was a delicious little nub that demanded to be sated. I would give Stella what she wanted, what she needed.

I swirled the tip of my index finger around her clit and rubbed it in increasingly strong strokes. She was going wild, her hips meeting my movements with more and more urgency. She ground against me, begging for a release she wouldn't get until every inch of me was buried in her tight heat.

I brought my wet fingers to my mouth and licked her sweetness from them.

She watched, her eyes glazed with lust, just like I wanted her.

I slid my cock to her opening. Her flesh was no longer hot, but molten. The muscles along my back shook with the need to plunge into her, to take what I wanted just as roughly as I wanted it. I couldn't. I wouldn't hurt her. Not this time. Not yet.

"Sinclair." It was a reverent prayer from her bruised lips.

I pushed inside, my head squeezing into her exquisite velvet. She moaned and clutched at my chest. I couldn't tell if she wanted to push me away or pull me closer. Either way, I couldn't stop. I needed her more than I'd ever needed anything in my life. I watched as I fed myself slowly into her, inch by inch. Further in, then out, then even further. When I was seated as deeply as I could go, her muscles clenched around me, pulling me farther inside. Still, I wanted more. I wanted it all.

I wrenched her hands above her head and pinned them as I drew back and filled her completely.

"Fuck."

"Sinclair, please."

I had never heard a sexier sound in my life.

"Please what?"

She rubbed up against me, her clit begging for release just as her mouth did.

"Please just, just…I want to come."

Fuck. My cock pulsed inside her, perilously close to the edge. I steadied my breathing.

"Do you want me to make you come, Stella?"

"Yes."

I pulled out and slid all the way back in before starting a slow rhythm. Her face was a mix of pleasure and pain as I slowly made her mine.

"Look at me, Stella."

Her eyes were half mast, but locked on mine all the same. I wanted her to watch me as I brought her pleasure. The fucking barbarian who lived in my breast demanded it, demanded that she acknowledge I was the only one who could give her the release she was begging for.

I licked into her open lips before taking her mouth again. I claimed her fully, my cock and my tongue embedded in her and giving her gratification. I knew my seed was close to bursting, my balls drawn up tight against me. I wouldn't come, not until she did. Once I felt her muscles milking me, I would coat her pussy lips. The picture in my mind almost sent me over the edge.

I pulled out to my tip and kissed down to her hard nipple. When I released her hands, she put them in my hair, pulling until it hurt and I growled against her tender flesh. I bit down on her nipple and fucked her harder, ramming my cock deep into her. Her hips rose up to meet me, marking my rhythm.

I knew she was close, the tension building in her as I'd intended. Each shuddering thrust went right to her clit.

She arched off the couch, her gorgeous breasts shaking from my impacts as she rubbed her clit into me stroke for stroke.

"Don't stop! Please, Sinclair. Don't stop." Her voice was sex, raw and low.

As if I had a choice. There was no stopping, not now, not when I was so deep in her slick pink.

"Come for me, Stella. I own this body. Now I want it to come."

"Sinclair." She thrashed her head from side to side.

I couldn't tell if she was refusing me or lost in her own passion. Either way, she needed to focus on me. I gripped her hair and forced her to meet my eyes.

I plunged into her, my skin slapping into her with each vicious strike. The sound reverberated around the room. I fucked her like an animal, vicious and base. Her moans spurred me on harder and faster.

I gripped her hair tightly, the fine strands catching on my fingers. I wanted her to feel nothing but me, think nothing but me. "You're mine. Come for me Stella. Now."

At my words, her pussy convulsed and she cried out my name in a river of release. The sound was unbearable. I pulled from her and lashed her clenching flesh with ropes of cum. My release was ripped from me, my body seizing from head to toe as I fisted my length and coated her with my seed. Her gaze was fastened on me as I came. There in her eyes was something I never even imagined to see. It was possessive, proud even.

When my last ounce of cum rested on her perfect skin, I sat up and let my head fall back. I gulped in deep breaths as she panted beneath me.

"That was, that was…" She sputtered beneath me, her eyes glassy.

"I know," I said.

As I stared at the ceiling, invisible guilt and responsibility crashed down on me. What had I done? Weren't things already complicated enough?

"Don't do that." Her voice was soft now, the release liquefying her tension.

"Do what?"

"Regret it. Regret me."

How could I not?

A sound like a gunshot echoed around the room, then another. I snapped my head back down. Lucius stood in the doorway, slow clapping. I fell back, grabbed my coat from the floor, and covered Stella.

"Very nice, big bro. I'm going to have to go rub one out after that."

Stella covered her face with both hands.

"Don't be shy, Stella. I really enjoyed the whole show. Your tits are, in a word, epic. And I can only imagine how sweet that pussy is for Sin here to bust a nut so quickly."

"Get out." I stood and yanked my pants up.

"I was just up for a midnight snack, is all. You can't blame me for making sure there wasn't a burglar. You know, the kind that fucks really loudly before robbing the place blind." He smirked. I hated it, mostly because it was almost the perfect mirror of mine.

I advanced on him. He backed away laughing. "I'm going. Because, seriously, going to have to stroke it before I can even think of sleeping again. I'll, of course, have to replace you with me in the reenactment, but I'm sure you understand."

I stalked toward him, ready to murder my own blood. How fitting.

He turned on his heel and disappeared down the hallway, his smug laugh shredding my already non-existent composure.

I returned to Stella and used my coat to clean her off. She draped an arm over her tits and then pushed her skirt down to cover herself. When she sat up and turned to get her shirt, I saw the scars on her back.

My guts wrenched, the memory of that night making my stomach churn and bile rise into my throat. So much pain. Her blood had soaked into my clothes. As soon as the spotlight was gone and the ballgoers' attention was turned elsewhere, I'd carried her out, clutched closely to my breast. I couldn't bear for anyone else to touch her, look at her. Her blood soaked through the vining cloak, painting everything a gruesome crimson and scenting the air with copper.

Her blood still covered my hands, though only I could see it. And now I'd taken even more from her. Remorse wasn't an option for me, not anymore. I'd set out to be this, to do this, to become the monster I had to be.

I reached out and ran my hand across one of the marks. She froze and glared at me over her shoulder. The accusation in her eyes was warranted, more than fair. It still struck me hard, embedding in my chest and spreading its barbs into my heart.

She yanked her top down, hiding what I'd done to her. Her cheeks were red, shame or some other emotion tingeing them with rose.

"It's time for you to make good on your promise. I want to see my father and stepbrother."

"What? Now?" I hadn't seen that coming. I should have.

"Yes. You said you'd arrange it when I asked. So, I'm asking."

I didn't want them here, poisoning her against me. Though that was a ridiculous thought. I was doing it plenty well on my own.

She bristled at my hesitation. "Well, are you going to be true to your word or not?"

My mother would have struck her for such an impertinent question. I didn't move. "I'm always true to my word. What day would you like to see them?"

"Tomorrow, in the afternoon."

"Fine, but only for an hour. No more."

"An hour? That's not enough time t-to—"

"I never promised you how long they could visit, I just

agreed that they could." I hated the thought of her stepbrother here, speaking to her, thinking he had any sway over her. He didn't. He never would again.

She stood and smoothed her skirt down with quick, angry movements. "You know what? I was wrong before. You should regret it. You should regret all of it."

She left, never looking back and taking more of me with her than I should have allowed.

CHAPTER SIXTEEN
STELLA

I FIDGETED WITH my hair, pulling it to the back and ensuring it covered the tattoo. I didn't want Dad or Dylan seeing the permanent brand. I wore a simple black sweater and a gray skirt. To their eyes, I would no doubt look the same as I had a month ago. Only I knew that the woman they remembered was long gone.

The front door opened and footsteps approached. I stood, nerves making my movements jerky. I was desperate to see my father, but I worried he would get too worked up. He didn't need to suffer any more than necessary.

Dad rushed in and embraced me. I didn't realize my tears were falling until they rolled down to my lips, salty on my tongue.

"Daddy," was all I could choke out.

Dylan stood a few steps back, bowed up with rage. Vinemont stood behind them, leaning against the wide doorway into the sitting room.

My father held me for the longest time. He stroked my hair and kept saying he was sorry.

I pulled away and looked into his watery blue eyes.

"Don't be sorry. I chose to do this. I would do anything to keep you safe."

He shook his head, now covered in even more gray than I remembered. "That's what I'm supposed to do. Not you."

"We're going to get you out of here, Stella." Dylan crushed me in his thick arms, squeezing me to him.

"I will get you back," he whispered in my ear.

I rested my chin on his shoulder and caught Vinemont staring daggers at Dylan.

Jealous, Vinemont?

I placed a chaste kiss on Dylan's cheek and glanced at Vinemont. He fisted his hands at his sides, the impeccable suit and tie he wore doing a poor job of hiding the animal underneath.

Dylan set me back and looked me up and down. "Has he hurt you?"

"I-I—"

Dylan whirled and advanced on Vinemont who just stood and smirked. He was taunting Dylan, drawing him in so he could hurt him. I knew the power in Vinemont's body, the way he could break even a man like Dylan.

"No one has hurt me," I lied. "Please, just, let's just sit down. We only have an hour. Please."

He stopped only a few feet from Vinemont, and the men engaged in a testosterone-laden stare down. I went to Dylan and tried to pull him away.

"Come on, Dylan. Sit with me."

He laid a hand over mine and an arm around my waist. Vinemont crossed his arms over his chest, muscles popping even through his dress shirt.

I led Dylan away before my hour was stolen with pointless violence. I'd already had enough of that for a lifetime.

Dad sank down in a fluffy side chair as Dylan and I sat on the floral sofa. Sun poured into the room, belying the chilly air outside. My father was thinner, though he seemed well put together, his clothes new and pressed. Dylan wore his usual rugby shirt and jeans.

Vinemont didn't move from the door. I glared up at him, willing him away. He smiled back, daring me to ask him to leave. I knew it was useless. Instead, I put my hand in Dylan's and laced our fingers together.

Enjoy the show, asshole.

From the corner of my eye, I saw him shift from one foot to the other, tension in his taut muscles. I'd seen them, intimately, closely. I brushed those thoughts away and focused on my father.

"How have you been?"

He looked at the floor before bringing his gaze back to mine. "I know I keep saying it, but I'm sorry. I should have just let him lock me up. I should have... You never should have come here."

"I don't want to talk about should haves or could haves. We only have a short time and I want to hear about you. How's the house? Have you had any more trouble from your old clients? Did any of my paintings sell?"

I forced a smile to my face, encouraging my father to engage with me like we were normal human beings, not as a grieving father and an enslaved daughter.

"Oh, your paintings." He almost managed a smile. "Yes, yes. The gallery called. Just a few days ago, some highbrow collector came in and bought every last one of your works."

"Someone bought out the gallery?"

"No, not the whole gallery, just your pieces. It was the damnedest thing. Paid full for each one and had them shipped. I don't know who it was, and the gallery kept their information confidential. But the check was real enough." His gaze dropped again. "I put it in your account. It'll be there when you get back."

My heart soared at the thought of my art gracing some collector's walls. I'd never sold more than a few paintings every so often. Certainly, no one had ever bought two at once. This news was like Christmas… Then I remembered what my real Christmas would entail.

My smile faltered a bit before I plastered it back across my face. "Dylan, how's school?"

"Same old, same old. My lacrosse team is leading the SEC like it does every year…" He gave the broad strokes of his life outside, the start of a new school year. Instead of making me feel better, it only reinforced my isolation here at the Vinemont estate.

I resolved to get outdoors more, especially now that my back had healed. Renee had spoken of stables on the property. I'd always been a decent rider.

When Dylan wound down, my father leaned forward and took my hands. "Please tell me what you've been doing for the past month. I think about you every moment."

I glanced to Vinemont. His gaze bored into me.

"I mostly stay in the house. I read and paint. There are others here. I have a good friend, Renee. And Vinemont's brothers are pleasant, especially the youngest, Teddy." Okay, I may have fibbed a bit—well, a lot—but I couldn't exactly explain that I was whipped bloody and paraded around naked.

"Has he hurt you? Has anyone? I couldn't bear to think of them hurting you." The tears welled in Dad's eyes again.

I shook my head in vehement denial. "No, no. They're all very nice here. I'm fine, really. It's like an upscale prison, really. Food's good, too. Far better than anything you ever made, Dad."

That would have made him laugh a month ago. Now, though, he only smiled sadly.

"If they just keep you around as a pet, what's the point?" Dylan asked.

"I, um, I don't really know." Lies were rolling off my tongue more easily by the minute. "I think it's just some sort of traditional thing they do here."

"Why don't you enlighten us, asshole?" Dylan turned

to Vinemont.

"Oh, suffice it to say, I like owning beautiful things. As you know, your stepsister is particularly lovely, especially when unencumbered with trifles like clothing." Vinemont didn't miss a beat.

I gripped Dylan's hand hard, keeping him next to me on the couch instead of challenging the devil in the doorway.

"I have an idea, Stella. Why don't you show Dylan who you belong to?"

Ice water flowed through my heart. "What?"

"If he wants to know why I keep you and what I do to you, just give him a peek at your neck. I realize he's slow, but maybe a little demonstration will help him figure it out."

Dylan was already searching my throat with his gaze. "What's he talking about, Stella?"

"Nothing." I smoothed my hair down.

"Did he do something to you?" Dad asked. The sadness in his voice broke off a piece of my heart, leaving a bloody, jagged edge.

"No, he's just talking."

"Show them, Stella." It was a command now, no longer a suggestion.

"No." I pleaded with him, humiliation rising to color my cheeks.

"Is this a road you want to go down?" Vinemont looked from my father to me, the threat lingering in the air. "Do it."

"Don't talk to her like that." Dylan's anger mixed with the already-dangerous current of emotions in the room.

"No, I'll show you. Just don't antagonize him."

"I'm not scared of him." Dylan rose and faced Vinemont. "Of *you*. Let's take this outside, motherfucker."

"Wait, no, Dylan. He's right. He owns me. I let him, okay? I'm his. Look." I bent my head and pulled my hair to the side. "See? I'm his. I chose to be here, chose to be his."

My father gasped. "No, Stella."

"See, *Dylan?*" Vinemont's self-satisfied tone made me want to claw his eyes out.

"All I see is a pussy who gets his rocks off hurting women," Dylan snarled.

Score one for Dylan.

"Let's not be so reductive. I enjoy hurting men, too, especially dumb brutes like you. Want me to show you?" Vinemont pushed off the doorframe and stood at the ready.

I smoothed my hair back over the mark. "Stop, both of you! Dylan, please, for me, just talk to me a while longer. Ignore him. Don't you see? He wants you to go outside and fight him."

"Time's wasting, Dylan," Vinemont added not-so-helpfully.

Dad dropped his head in his hands. I'd never seen him so defeated. I sank to my knees at his feet. "Please don't, Dad. It's going to be okay. All of it. Eleven months left? That's nothing. I'll be back before you know it."

"I'll never forgive myself." He shuddered as a sob ripped through him.

"There's nothing to forgive," I said. "Please don't torture yourself. I want you to be healthy and happy when I come home. I want you to be waiting for me with open arms. I'll be there, Daddy. You'll see. It's not that long at all." I pressed my forehead to his.

He offered no more words as his tears overcame him. I wrapped my arms around his shaking frame. I pulled from some deep well of strength inside myself—one I didn't even know was there—as I held him.

"Time's up." Vinemont scowled at us.

"Look at him! Do you truly have no heart?" I hissed.

"In this case? No. No, I don't. Now, gents, I suggest you get the fuck out of my house."

"And if we don't?" Dylan asked.

"Lucius," Vinemont called.

His brother appeared, the two of them presenting a solid wall of muscle. They were almost a matching set. Both were glowering, their threat palpable. They could beat Dylan and my father senseless, and they would if given the opportunity.

"I'll walk you out. Come on." I refused to allow them to hurt Dad or Dylan.

My father rose with difficulty, and I helped him to the front door. Dylan took his other elbow as we maneuvered down the front steps. A black BMW waited out front.

"Did your mom get you a new car?" I asked.

"No, it's his." Dylan gestured to Dad.

"Oh." I supposed his old, beat up Camry finally died.

I gave Dad another long hug. "I'll see you again soon. I promise."

He put a shaking hand to my cheek. "I'll count the moments."

Vinemont snorted as if Dad had told a joke. I shot him a corrosive glare.

Dylan and I helped Dad into the driver's seat. Once he was in, I gave Dylan a long hug. Both Vinemont and Lucius smirked, no doubt feeling like they'd won some sort of victory. I'd show them.

When Dylan pulled away, I stood on my tiptoes and kissed him on the mouth. At first he was surprised, but then he deepened it, bending me back and clutching me to him. His tongue sank in my mouth, trying to get the fullest taste possible. It wasn't exactly enjoyable, but when he pulled me back upright and I broke the embrace, the fire in the Vinemont brothers' eyes was more than worth it.

"That was…" Dylan ran a hand through his hay-colored locks. "That was nice."

"I'll see you again soon." I put my hand on his chest, playing it up like an Oscar was hanging in the balance.

He sobered. "I'll get you out of here. I swear I will."

I smiled at him, though I knew his oath would be

broken. There was no getting out of here. Not for me. Not until my time was up.

Dylan walked to the passenger side and dropped in. I waved them away down the driveway. When the car disappeared in the glare of the sun, I turned and floated back up the stairs.

Vinemont grabbed my arm. "What was that?"

"What?" I fluttered my lashes innocently.

"You know what."

I shrugged, enjoying the muscle ticking in his jaw. "I'm just an affectionate stepsister. What can I say?" I pulled my arm from his grasp and strode past an equally pissed Lucius.

"Good afternoon, boys," I called, and closed the front door behind me, my heart full to bursting with my petty victory.

CHAPTER SEVENTEEN
STELLA

THE NEXT MORNING, I breakfasted with Teddy. He was back from school for the weekend. We actually had a long discussion about his art appreciation class. Like Lucius, he seemed to have an eye for good art.

He started out throwing major shade at Jackson Pollack, but by the end of his second coffee, he was coming around to the idea that all art didn't have to be still lifes and flowers in vases. I was growing fonder of him despite myself. He seemed so normal, like a young man trying to figure himself out and make his way in the world.

I wondered how such a well-adjusted person could have come from the likes of the Vinemont family. Then again, I'd only ever met Lucius and Sinclair. I didn't know what their parents had been like.

"So, now that we've gotten your art classes straightened out," I said, "I have a few questions of my own. I'm tired of being cooped up in here, and I think you can help me out. Are there horses I could ride?"

"Like here, on the estate?" He tore through a piece of bacon and winked at the pretty maid as she refilled my cup.

"Yeah."

"Sure. I'll take you. I can't ride with you, though. I have to finish some homework, and then I have a date." His gaze slid back to the maid, Laura.

"Oh? Something romantic?" I asked.

"We'll see." He stood. "Come on."

I followed him out to the hallway.

"Hang on, Stella. You can't wear tennis shoes to ride. Got any boots?"

I looked down at my outfit. "You're right. I'll meet you back here in five minutes."

I rushed upstairs and threw on some jeans, a t-shirt, a light jacket, and boots before returning to Teddy. Laura scurried away when I hit the bottom step. Teddy smiled, his lips a little redder than they were when I left him.

"Don't say anything to Sin, okay?" He led me through the kitchen and then out through a back hallway.

"I don't intend to say anything to him, period. So that should be easy."

"Yeah, you two have some kind of crazy thing going on. I don't really understand it. I've learned just to not ask any questions anymore. They don't tell me anything, anyway." He shrugged. His hair was lighter than Vinemont's but he was just as tall and almost as built. It was no wonder Laura had taken a liking to him.

He led me to some sort of ATV that was parked behind the house and motioned for me to get on the back. He swung a leg over and cranked it up.

"Where are the, um, helmets?" I asked over the sound of the engine.

"Scared?" He smiled, and I realized he was a lady killer hidden in the body of a young, sweet man.

I snugged up behind him and wrapped my arms around his middle. "Go fast."

He laughed, a deep rumble I could feel through his back.

"Yes, ma'am."

The day was uncharacteristically warm, but the breeze created by the speeding ATV was delicious. The smell of fall was in the air, crisp and familiar. Many trees still bore some seasonal color, while others had already given up, their branches bare and dormant.

He gunned it down the curving drive. I squealed with the pleasure of movement and freedom. The barn loomed up ahead, large and classically red. Bales of hay were lined up out front, and chickens pecked around from a nearby coop. It was a lovely picture, really—the sky mostly blue with a few fluffy clouds, the red of the barn, and the color in the trees, all working together to create something idyllic.

We flew past the barn and came to the stables, painted the same iconic red. He parked out front and helped me off the ATV.

"That was fun."

He smiled again, beautiful. "Anytime. I'll get you set up. Come on."

We went into the stables and he disappeared into what I assumed was the tack room. There were several horses in the expansive enclosure. Two struck my fancy. One, large and dark. He nickered at me in greeting. I held out my hand and rubbed his nose lightly. He was proud but still friendly.

The next was a white mare, so light she looked almost silver. She watched me approach and nuzzled my hand.

"Oh, you've gone for Gloria. She's my favorite. I would have picked her for you, myself."

"Do you take care of the horses all the time?"

"No. I'd love to, though. Just don't have the time with school. We have a stable master and a few grooms. They keep the horses and take them to shows and things like that. They're out at a show right now. Should be back tomorrow."

Teddy carried a saddle to Gloria's stall.

"Come on Gloria, how does a nice ride sound?" She

nickered and nodded her head.

I laughed. "She certainly knows how to get her point across."

"You'll never meet a smarter horse." He threw a glance over his shoulder at the black gelding. "No offense, Shadow."

Shadow didn't respond.

"That's Sin's horse," he explained.

"I should have guessed."

Teddy led Gloria from the stall and got her all set up for me. Once the bridle was set, he helped me up and adjusted the stirrups.

"Feel good?" He ran a hand down Gloria's mane.

"Yep. I think this is just right. Thanks, Teddy." I loved being astride a horse. It made me feel so tall, powerful.

"My pleasure." He led Gloria and me from the shady stables out into the dappled light.

"Now, like I said, I don't know the deal, but I'm pretty sure I'd be in big trouble if you rode off into the sunset and never came back." He squinted up at me.

"Not on your watch, Teddy. I promise."

"All right then. Head that way if you want to ride past the lake and over the levee. There are some pulp woods over there if you want trees above you, or you could ride back toward the house. It's up to you."

"I think I'll see the lake."

"Good choice." He looked up. "Don't stay out here too long. When it's warm like this, storms aren't far behind."

"I won't. It's been a long time since I've ridden. My ass will be sore in no time." I blushed. *What did I just say?*

He chuckled. "Fair enough."

I set off at a slow trot, following the road. Teddy roared off on his ATV back to the house. I hoped his date went well.

He was right about the day being unseasonably warm. I shed my jacket and tied it around my waist. I spurred

Gloria on a little faster and she was happy to oblige. Maybe she'd been cooped up for too long, just like me. She was a smooth ride, her pace perfect. Someone had clearly loved on her and trained her well.

Before long, we were racing through the grass. The wind whipped against my face and my hair flew out behind me. I loved every second of it. Fear mixed with exhilaration as I leaned down and gripped her mane. The sun bathed my face in light and delicious heat.

We'd sped for miles, the stables long gone and only the encroaching woods and the thinner strip of grass next to the road in our view. Out here, away from the house, the grounds were far less manicured, the grass high and wild.

We startled some deer in an open field as we hurtled past, sending them scattering for the trees, their white tails up in alarm. Gloria didn't seem to mind. She powered ahead, free and fast, the wind a song of liberation in our ears.

After a few more minutes of a full-on gallop, I pulled back on the reins, slowing her down and sitting back upright. I guided her back onto the road and we clip-clopped over a bridge spanning a wide bayou branch. Fish swam in the waters beneath us and frogs sang in the trees. A few hundred yards ahead I caught the sparkle of a large span of water. The levee. We trotted up to the edge. It was a sizeable reservoir, the lake disappearing into wooded inlets far off in the distance.

On the far edge, I could just make out the straight lines of a cottage in the woods.

"Think there are alligators in there, Gloria?"

She nickered and nipped at the high grass.

Cattails grew along the sides of the water and lilypads floated here and there. A ramshackle dock and small wooden boat were abandoned nearby. The water darkened toward the center. How deep was it?

I guided Gloria further up the bank where a small retaining pond split off from the larger lake. A grassy berm separated the bodies of water. At the top, I dismounted and dropped to the ground. The last few cicadas of the summer played their song in the pines that hemmed in the water on all sides. I always associated the sound with hot days.

I let Gloria eat the high grass as I lay out on the ground, staring up at the passing clouds. I popped in the stolen earbuds and set Lucius' iPod to random, listening to his eclectic mix of music as the sun smiled down, warming me with comforting beams.

I laced my fingers behind my head and closed my eyes.

Gloria's loud whinny woke me. I must have dozed off in the warm sun. It was gone now, dark clouds hovering above, promising a downpour. A rumble of thunder had Gloria nuzzling at my head with her nose.

I got to my knees and then stood. "I'm up. I'm up. We'd better get back."

I stowed the purloined iPod. As I clambered onto Gloria's back, the clouds erupted, huge raindrops pelting us. Then the hail came, larger than anything that should ever fall from the sky. The size of golf balls, the ice hurt with each stinging impact. It would take half an hour, likely more, to get back to the stables. The only other shelter was the cottage in the woods I'd spotted earlier. I couldn't see it anymore for the curtains of rain and the pelting hail, but it wasn't far.

A piece struck my forehead and I felt warm blood running down my face.

Shit.

I couldn't stay out in the open. I made my decision and urged Gloria toward the woods. We would have to ride the storm out in the cottage. The thunder grew louder, the booming reverberating in my chest as lightning streaked across the sky.

We made it to the tree line, the branches above blocking out or at least slowing down the balls of hail. Gloria whinnied as a streak of lightning led to a deafening crack of thunder. I stroked her mane.

"It's okay, girl. We just have to make it to the cottage."

I led her through the trees, heading to where I remembered the cottage sat. Or at least I thought I was. We were in the heart of the storm, gloom and sheets of rain cutting visibility down to nearly nothing.

I urged her on. The cottage had to be nearby. I hoped I hadn't missed it in the murky woods. We went a little farther, but there was still no sign of the cottage. We must have just passed it. I turned Gloria around to double back.

The rain seemed to let up a little bit, a brief respite. Maybe the storm was passing and we could head back to the stables instead of trying to ride it out? Then, a strange sensation shot through my body, like a tingling. *Oh, no.*

"Gloria, go!" I cried.

Too late. Lightning struck so near us that Gloria reared back and threw me. I hit a tree trunk. The deafening boom of thunder was the last thing I heard.

CHAPTER EIGHTEEN
SINCLAIR

I MADE IT to the front porch before a heavy rain began to fall. Then came the hail. Good thing I'd parked in the garage. Once inside, I pulled my coat off and handed it to Farns before loosening my tie.

"She in the library?" I asked.

"No, Mr. Sinclair. I believe she and Teddy went out for a ride."

"Not smart." Teddy would take care of her, at least. An image of Stella in a wet t-shirt floated through my mind. The thought of her with Teddy was no longer so palatable. "I guess I'll go see if they made it out of the rain."

"Very good, sir." Farns smiled.

I climbed the stairs two at a time to my room. I stripped out of my suit and dressed in a t-shirt and jeans. I was ripping a raincoat from its hanger when a rhythmic banging wafted to my ears.

Lucius was still at the plant. I'd spoken to him on the phone, so no one else should have been in our wing of the house. I yanked on some boots and headed down the hall, creeping along the runner so my steps were silent.

The closer I got to Teddy's room, the louder the sound

grew, and it was interspersed with grunts and feminine moans. My hands clenched. Fire laced around my heart, squeezing like a lasso of flames, drawing me inexorably closer to his door. The image of Stella was back, but this time she was beneath Teddy, writhing in pleasure as he fucked her. I had to lean a hand on the wall as my sight grew hazy, rage coloring everything a shade darker.

No. Well, Farns did say they'd gone for a ride. I would have laughed if anything were funny. Nothing was. Murder might be entertaining, but definitely not amusing. I gripped the door handle, steeling myself for what I was about to see. The cries grew louder and beneath them was the sound of skin slapping on skin.

I flung the door open. Teddy was on top of the maid from the kitchen, Laura. He rolled off her when he saw me.

"Sin!" Teddy threw his blanket across her naked body.

I let out a pent up breath. Relief washed through me, replacing the bitter taste of hate and rage.

"Don't you fucking knock anymore?"

"Fuck, Teddy. I thought you were…" I shook my head.

"With Stella?" Teddy asked.

"I should go." Laura's voice quavered.

"No, stay." Teddy smoothed a hand over her knee.

Her face looked pinched as she stared up at me.

I sighed. "I'm not going to fire you, Laura." *Though I should.*

I should have ordered her to pack up and leave then and there. Instead, my mind was whirring away with where Stella was, what she was doing. Teddy's discipline could wait.

She let out a pent up breath, the blood returning to her face with a vengeance.

"Of course he's not going to fire you." Teddy glared at me.

"Teddy. We've talked about this. You can't fuck the help."

"Just like you can't fuck the Acquisition?"

I returned his glare. "Stella is none of your business. I told you to stay out of it."

"It's kind of hard for me to stay out of it when you force her to stand naked on the table or whip her so badly—"

"Teddy!" I barked. I glanced to Laura. She looked away, pretending to be deaf.

He shrugged and dropped his gaze. "You know what I mean."

"Teddy, please believe me when I tell you that you don't know shit about any of it. Not the Acquisition, and definitely not Stella." I regretted the words as soon as they were out. Teddy looked stung. Lucius was fair game, but Teddy—he wasn't like us. He had a good heart.

I balled my anger up and pushed it down before resuming in an even tone. "I'm sorry, Teddy. I didn't mean it that way."

"I'd know more about it if you'd tell me. Maybe I could help." He stood and ran a hand through his hair. He didn't seem to notice his half-mast dick was waving around.

"You don't need to know. It's only for the firstborn." I'd had this conversation about six times with him ever since Stella arrived.

"Then why does Lucius know?"

"Lucius just thinks he knows. He doesn't. Trust me. When you're older and if you have to deal with this shit, you'll know. And you'll regret it, okay?"

He grumbled and sat back down. He shot a glance to Laura and his demeanor brightened the slightest bit.

The silence became more than awkward. Laura coughed.

"So, where's Stella?" The question that had been on my lips from the moment I walked in the door finally broke free.

"She went for a ride." Teddy turned to look out the window. "Shit. I didn't realize that was thunder I was hearing. I thought it was—"

"Your bed busting through the wall, stallion?" I needed to break the tension. Teddy was worth protecting and I didn't want him to feel like I did—caught in an unfair trap.

He smiled, blushing. "Something like that."

I followed his gaze out into the downpour.

Fuck. If Stella was out in this, she'd be soaked through and lucky if she avoided the hail. The temperature was dropping now that the cold front was moving through. I needed to find her. Fast.

"She was heading to the levee, if that helps," Teddy said.

"It does. Thanks, Ted. Sorry for the interruption."

I swung the door closed. As I hit the stairs, the rhythm began wafting from his room again.

I dashed to the garage and started my car. The rain was a milky barrier and the hail pinged off the luxury vehicle. It was painful hearing the damage, but I was too worried to care. I broke through the sheets of opaque water and raced down the slick drive into the back part of the estate. I contemplated driving down toward the levee, but realized if I did and she'd gone off in the woods, I wouldn't be able to find her. I pulled up into the stables and killed the engine.

I hoped she was inside, warm and dry, waiting for the rain to stop. I ran down the stalls, looking for her. She wasn't there, and the mare Gloria was gone. Something unsettling and queasy swirled in my stomach. It was a feeling I wasn't very familiar with, not anymore. Fear.

Shadow whinnied at a particularly loud blast of thunder and stomped his disapproval. The tack room door was open and a saddle was missing. I wasted no time getting my horse saddled and ready. He stood calmly as the thunder rumbled, as if desperate to get out for a ride, storm be damned.

"It's going to be a wet trip." I climbed into the saddle and spurred him out of the stables and into the rain. At least the hail had stopped.

The droplets stung as I urged Shadow into the deluge. We set a hellish pace. It wasn't simply raining, the sky was jettisoning the water, throwing it forcefully earthward. Lightning split the sky above us, the flash and resulting sound making Shadow rear.

"Steady. Steady, boy." I held onto the reins for dear life and eased him back down. "Keep it together." I ran my hand along his nape, smoothing his mane as the rain soaked through me, the jacket doing nothing against the onslaught.

He resumed a moderate gallop, and I guided him onto the road as the grass along the sides became muck. It was harder on his hooves, but made it easier for him to maneuver, so he picked up his pace. I felt as if I were racing the clock—a burning need to get to Stella had settled deep in my gut.

What was she thinking going for a ride alone? If she wanted to ride she should have asked me. I would have taken her. Now, she'd gotten herself into a mess. Even as I silently berated her, that same queasy fear overcame my ire.

I saw movement in the gloomy sheets of rain ahead. A horse. My heart rose. I pulled back on the reins. I could lead Stella back to the stables and get her warmed up in no time. I ignored the intense relief that settled over me and squinted against the wall of water. A gust of wind pushed the watery curtain aside for a split second. My heart sank.

Fuck.

Gloria emerged from the downpour and flew past us, back toward the stables. She was riderless and beyond spooked. My momentary reprieve sent me into an even deeper state of panic once I realized it was nothing more than a mirage. Stella was somewhere out in the storm.

My thoughts came in a torrent to match the deluge all around me. Teddy said she went toward the levee. Where would she have wandered?

"Faster, Shadow." I dug my heels in and he shot forward.

I ignored the bite of the water droplets lashing my face. The cold was seeping into my pores, leeching away my body heat as I urged Shadow forward. The streaking lightning and rolling thunder became just another part of the blur of scenery. We were full gallop, a breakneck pace, racing into the heart of the raging storm.

We crossed the narrow bridge leading to the levee. I pulled him to the left, up to the top of the knoll where I felt Stella may have tarried. We slowed and turned in a circle around the area. She must have been here. I could barely see, but the grass had been chewed, and some of the blades were smoothed down, as if someone had lain there recently. She'd been here. Where did she go?

Though I couldn't see it, I knew the old hunting camp was nearby. She may have tried to make it to the log cabin. I spurred Shadow up and around the edge of the lake and into the pine woods. I kept a tight hold on the reins. Shadow was spooked, ready to bolt. I kept his gait slow. If Stella were trying to shelter under the branches, I couldn't afford to miss her. Shadow's feet were sinking in the muddy ground beneath the trees and he kept trying to move faster.

"Easy boy. Slow. Keep it slow." The roar of the rain hitting every surface stifled my voice, but Shadow obeyed.

I angled him toward where I knew the log cabin sat in the woods. We'd gone about a hundred yards before the smell of ozone overcame the fresh scent of water in the air. A blackened tree, scarred and hewn in two lay to our right. It must have been struck recently.

Shit. Where is she?

We cantered a little further before I saw her. She lay in a crumpled mass on the ground. My heart, already racing, felt like it could have stopped altogether, never to beat again. I jumped from Shadow, keeping a hard grip on the reins as I dragged him to her.

"Stella!" I yelled against the rain, my voice barely carrying above the howling wind.

She didn't move. Blood streamed from a wound along her brow and she was pale, far too white. I scooped her into my arms, the fear in my soul real, almost palpable.

She was breathing. When her chest moved against me, I carefully draped her limp body across Shadow's back. With one hand holding her secure and the other still squeezing the reins, I led Shadow through the trees, the rumbles of thunder no match for the booming beat of my heart. I pushed forward, ripping my boots from the soaked and muddy ground again and again. After a while, my legs burned from the effort. I ignored the pain. Nothing would stop me from getting her to safety. I kept pushing until the cabin came into view.

I pulled Shadow up onto the wide porch and fastened his reins to the railing. "You'll be safe here." I hoisted Stella from his back and carried her inside.

The cabin was old, but we kept it up. Recently remodeled with modern amenities, it was much more than a usual hunting camp. I tracked mud onto the Carrera marble floors and laid Stella, dirty and bloody, onto the leather sofa. The storm still raged outside, but the cabin was like a cocoon, muffling the raw fury of the elements.

We were soaked. I brushed matted hair from her face and examined the cut along her temple. It was shallow, but bleeding like a son of a bitch. I felt around through her hair and discovered a golf ball sized knot on the side of her head. *Fuck.*

"Stella, wake up for me. Stella?"

She shivered. I set to work stripping her, yanking her boots off first before getting her down to her bra and panties. I checked her over, looking for blood or any broken bones. The dread left me incrementally, each piece of her that was intact wicked it away.

She seemed fine except for her head. Which was the exact opposite of fine, really. More than anything, I needed to get her warm. I picked her up and lay her down on the fluffy rug in front of the fireplace. I grabbed the remote from the mantle and clicked on the flames, forcing them higher and higher until warmth rushed forward and onto us.

I hurriedly stripped my clothes and pulled her close, her back to my front as we lay in front of the roaring fire. I pulled her hair away from her face and smoothed it down.

"Stella, I need you to wake up for me." I ran my hand down her side. Her skin was clammy and cold despite the blast of heat.

I grabbed the edge of the rug and flung it over us. We were wrapped in sheepskin and directly in front of the fire. We would either warm up or burn to death.

"Come on, Stella." I needed her to be all right. I told myself it was because I needed her for the Acquisition. It was a lie. I wanted her. I cared for her. And wasn't that just a fucking problem of epic proportions.

I kept rubbing my hand down her side, willing my heat into her. Slowly, her skin warmed under my touch. She shifted, her eyelids fluttering, and I breathed a sigh that carried more angst than I knew I was capable of holding.

"Sinclair?"

"Yes. I'm here."

"What happened?"

"You'll have to tell me. I found you in the woods. How's your head?"

"It hurts." Her voice was small.

I put my hands on her shoulders and turned her around so she faced me. The cut had stopped bleeding, but red still remained along the edges of her hair and in her eyebrow. I ran my hand over the bump on her head. It seemed to have shrunk a bit. I tilted her chin up so I could look into her eyes. The pupils appeared to match. No concussion. Maybe.

I shook my head and pulled her closer to me so her head fell into the crook of my neck. "You are a mess."

"You should see the other guy."

I laughed. I hadn't actually laughed from pure amusement at anyone except for my brothers in so long it felt odd, but also right.

"Mmm, I don't think I've ever heard you laugh. Well, maybe you do whenever you're drowning puppies or something. I've just never heard it."

I nuzzled into her wet hair. "Puppy drowning is every Thursday. You'll just have to catch me at the right time."

She giggled and draped an arm over me. The air between us expanded, somehow becoming bigger, fuller; maybe even a little expectant. We were lying on a rug in front of a fire while the storm raged outside. We should be drinking wine and laughing and fucking. But this wasn't a romance or a fairy tale. She was my Acquisition.

"Stop thinking." She lifted her lips to mine and brushed against them softly. A delicious tease.

"I don't know if I can."

"If I can then you can. After all, I'm the captive, the slave, the Acquisition, the one you whip and humili—"

I claimed her mouth because, fuck, I wanted to and to shut her up. Hearing her recite my long list of sins was too much truth. At that moment in front of the fire, I wanted the fairy tale. I wanted to be her knight instead of her demon. I kissed her like I meant it, like I felt something more for her than ownership. I let myself go. Just this one time.

She answered with more verve than I had any right to deserve or expect. She had surprised me so many times over the past weeks that I should have been accustomed to it. I wasn't. When she brought her hand to my cheek and caressed it lovingly, I was caught up in her more than I could stand. I threw the rug from us and pulled her on top of me, never breaking our desperate kiss.

She straddled me, the fabric of her panties a maddening barrier between her delectable skin and mine. I unhooked her bra. She sat up and took it off, her nipples puckered and hard in the dancing firelight. I palmed her breasts, the weight of each perfect in my hands. She closed her eyes and dropped her head back as I touched and stroked and teased. I leaned up and caught one of the pearled tips in my mouth. She tasted like rain and sweat and sweetness. Perfection. I licked and sucked her in, rubbing the nub against my tongue. Her hips moved against my cock, giving me a glimpse of what awaited me beneath the fabric—hot, wet, and wanting.

I hooked my fingers in the side of her panties and ripped them. I did the same on the other side and yanked them from her. My cock jumped at the promise of euphoria her pussy offered. I knew it was tight, slick, perfect. She rubbed her needy clit over my shaft, giving herself a cheating pleasure just as she gave me the same. I wanted it all.

I gripped her hips and raised her. She wrapped her small hand around my cock. She'd gone from cold to scorching hot in moments, and her touch made me hiss.

"Fucking hell, Stella." I could barely get the words out through my gritted teeth.

She teased me, rubbing my head against her clit as her hips rocked against me. I wasn't waiting any more. I pulled her forward, positioning my head at her opening. When she slid down on my shaft, I groaned from the demanding need to thrust up into her. My fingertips dug into her soft hips. She gave me a sultry gaze, eyes green and partly hidden beneath her lashes. When she raised up and settled down again, pushing me as deeply as I could go, it took every ounce of willpower I had not to flip her over and fuck her hard and fast.

She leaned down over me, brushing her perfect tits against my chest. She set a slow rhythm, as if trying to get used to my length inside her. It wasn't enough. I thrust up into her, meeting her strokes with pure animal lust to take everything she had. She was panting, each breath hot between her parted lips. I spread one palm over her ass and fisted her hair with the other.

I crushed our mouths together as our bodies melded into one. She moaned and sped her pace, gliding back and forth on my shaft and rubbing her clit against me. I wanted it in my mouth, but my cock wouldn't relinquish her tight heat for anything. I was rough, claiming her mouth and pulling her hair. She dug her nails into my chest as she rode me, all reservations gone, surrendered to our mutual pleasure.

I couldn't wait any longer. I flipped her onto her back and spread her legs wide beneath me. I sat back and fed each inch into her flushed pussy. It was the hottest thing I'd ever seen, making my balls pull up even tighter against me.

"Fucking beautiful, Stella."

"Sin," she breathed.

She'd never called me that. I would put that one rasping word on replay in my mind every time I stroked off to thoughts of her tight body.

I rammed myself home, all gentleness gone. I needed her, all of her. She gasped as I lay on top of her and pistoned into her. She grabbed tight onto my shoulders as I fastened my mouth to her neck, the slight salt of her sweat delicious on my tongue. She dug her heels into my back as I ground my cock into her softest skin.

Her hips were pinned, but she still managed to push against me, adding even more roughness to our frantic fucking.

"You like that, Stella? My cock deep inside you?"

"God, yes," she cried.

"Not god, Stella." I gave her some longer, harder strokes, and my cock demanded I explode inside her.

"Sin." She arched her back, rubbing her tits against me.

"Better." I bent my head down and pulled a stiff nipple into my mouth, sucking it as I pounded into her.

She scored her hands through my hair. "I'm so close."

I grazed her nipple with my teeth before I raised my

head up to meet her lusty gaze. "Yeah?"

I smoothed my hand down her stomach and leaned back, watching her tits bounce beautifully with each impact. I pulled her hips further up to me so I could stay just as deep. Because I was a selfish asshole.

I put one hand on her hip to keep her pinned beneath me then licked my other thumb and pressed the pad against her clit.

She bucked when I touched her sensitive nub.

"Look at me, Stella. I want you to tell me when you come, and I want you to tell me who made you come."

She nodded and gasped when I increased the pressure on her clit, still fucking her hard. My cock demanded release. I wouldn't give in, not until she was clamping around me.

Her gaze locked on mine as I swirled my thumb around her clit in small circles. Her pussy pulsed, and I knew she was near the edge. I pushed her over, rubbing her clit faster until her wet walls tensed and squeezed.

"Sin!" She came with crushing pressure on my cock.

Her pussy convulsed as she gripped the rug and repeated that one word. My cock couldn't take any more, not when I had this beautiful sight before me and her cunt milking me. I gave a final hard thrust and groaned as I shot into her, deep and hard. I filled her, each hot kick of my cock a blissful release until I was spent.

I let myself fall on top of her, feeling her last shudders as I remained buried deep inside.

CHAPTER NINETEEN
STELLA

MY BODY WAS sated. My soul, bereft. What had I done? This man who had just given me the most erotic moment of my life was hell-bent on my destruction.

I turned my head toward the fire as he dropped light kisses along my neck. A traitor was here in this room, and she lived inside my breast. I thought I was playing the game, making Vinemont care about me enough to keep me safe. But an ache in my heart, one that told me I'd taken these stolen moments in too deeply, was an accusatory slap in my face.

I tried to lure him to me, to make him care. I'd done the opposite, and my heart was the one caught in the trap. Even now, I wanted to taste his lips again, to make him hard and wanting under my touch. I let out a deep breath.

"Stop." He dropped kisses along my jaw.

"Stop what?"

"Thinking." He took my mouth again, gentle now, reverent.

I wanted him so much it twisted my heart. I wanted him to want me, to treasure me. But he'd always been upfront. Hell, he'd even told me he would gladly torture me all over again. He swept his tongue into my mouth, trying to erase all thought from my mind and nearly accomplishing it. His scent was all over me, marking me as his. I loved it and hated it at once.

I broke the kiss before I fell back under his spell. "I can't."

"My dick is still inside you, Stella, and now you can't?" He moved his hips for emphasis, sending a thrill back to my clit.

I pushed on his chest and he withdrew, pulling from me. I wanted him back immediately. He took in my body, the bruises coloring my nipples where he'd bitten me, the marks on my neck, his fingertips imprinted on my hips. He still looked hungry. I wanted to feed him.

I couldn't.

I pulled the fluffy rug up to my chest. He met my eyes.

"This was a mistake," I said.

"I know." He searched around, found his boxers, and pulled them on.

His words stung me more than they should have. The heat from the fire was oppressive now. He grabbed a remote and turned it down to a low flame. He ran a hand through his hair in what I now recognized as the classic "Vinemont man in distress" move.

"This can't happen again," he said. "None of it. We just have to make it through the year. That's all." He put a resolve into his words that I knew he didn't feel. "This was just…circumstances." He waved a hand at the windows where sunlight now poured through.

More pain bloomed in my chest. I ignored it because he was right. I was still his Acquisition, his plaything. He was still my captor. I dropped the rug and searched around for my clothes. He stared hard at my bare skin before looking away, his jaw tight.

The fire had mostly dried my clothes except for my jeans. I pulled them on anyway. He dressed, too, his movements quick and angry.

He led me through the front door.

Shadow stood on the front porch, his head almost brushing the rafters. He nickered as we emerged and nuzzled Vinemont's hand. He was so gentle with the animal, obvious affection in his touches. Shadow responded, resting his head on Vinemont's shoulder. They were a gorgeous set, dark and handsome.

Vinemont led him down the steps and into the wet grass. I followed, and Vinemont helped me up before seating himself behind me.

"Come on, Shadow, let's go home."

We rode in silence. A cold breeze had kicked up in the wake of the storm. Winter wouldn't be far behind. I lay back into Vinemont for warmth, or so I told myself. He wrapped his arms around me, keeping at least some of the chill wind at bay. Shadow maintained an easy pace, none of us seeming to be in a hurry to return.

My thoughts couldn't seem to focus on anything other than the man at my back, his actions and words. I still wanted to believe something was different between us. That our stolen moments in the library and at the cottage meant something more than just sex.

I wondered what was going through his mind. Was he worrying just like I was? He was unreadable at best. I relaxed back into him more, snuggling against his hard chest. He pulled me in closer, barely holding the reins as Shadow leisurely walked home.

As we approached the stables, I remembered my own horse that had bolted.

"Gloria?"

"I'm sure she's munching on some hay inside. She galloped past us in the thick of the downpour."

The storm, my accident – Vinemont had seen me through all of it. "Thanks, by the way."

"For what?"

"For…well, for saving me."

He leaned away. "I didn't. I haven't."

He pulled his arms from around me, letting the outside chill seep into my bones for the short distance before we trotted into the stables.

We skirted a sleek black car, still wet and slightly dinged. Gloria waited there, just as he'd said, grazing on a hay bale.

Vinemont dropped to the ground and then helped me down. He dug in his pocket and handed me his car key. "Take it back to the house. I need to get Gloria and Shadow settled. You need to warm up."

"I can stay and—"

"No. Just go." It was a dismissal. He turned his back and started unburdening Shadow.

Asshole. I opened the fancy car's door and slid into the driver's seat. I glanced down at the transmission. It was a stick. I hadn't driven a stick in years and wasn't much good at it to begin with. I smirked at Vinemont's broad back. This would hurt him more than it hurt me. I pushed the button on the ignition and the engine purred to life.

I depressed the clutch and easily put the car into reverse. I hit the gas and let off the clutch. It lurched forward and sputtered.

Not reverse.

Vinemont glanced over his shoulder and shook his head. I moved the gear shift into what was, most likely, reverse and tried it again. This time I slid backward out of the stables so quickly I had to slam on the brakes once I reached the smooth drive.

Vinemont had completely turned now, watching me with his arms crossed over his chest. I couldn't tell if he wore a look of chagrin or regret. Either way, I was going to make the next gear shift hurt. I ground it into first gear, the transmission screaming an angry noise, and hit the gas. I was off like a shot, leaving Vinemont and the stables behind me.

I moved it into second gear, imagining the look on

Vinemont's face as I ground that one even harder, the transmission making a vicious metal on metal sound. I smiled and whipped the rest of the way to the house. I parked out front, satisfied with myself.

Renee was sitting in the library and followed me up the stairs when I dashed in. I stripped in my room as she entered.

"Where have you been? What's happened?" Her curious gaze settled on my neck. "Are those love bites?"

"I, uh, I'm freezing. I need a bath and then I'll tell you about it."

She kicked into maid mode and ran me a hot bath while I tossed off my remaining clothes. As I soaked, letting the warmth soothe my aching body—some of the soreness from the riding accident, some of it from Vinemont's attentions—I told her about my day. I left out most of the sexy details, but she got the picture well enough.

The hand wringing began almost instantly. I closed my eyes and leaned my head back against the tub.

"Is it really as bad as all that, Renee?"

"Yes, and worse."

"Why?"

"If his mother finds out—"

My eyes shot open and I whipped my head around to her. She clapped her hand over her mouth.

"Vinemont's mother is *alive?* You told me she was dead!"

Epic hand wringing ensued. "I never said she was dead. You just drew your own conclusions."

Realization dawned. "The third floor?"

She nodded, a troubled look overcoming her features.

"Why does it matter? Where is she? Can she do anything about this, about the Acquisition?" My mind raced from thought to thought. Why was Vinemont's mother such a secret?

"It matters, and no, she can't help you. She wouldn't

even if she could. She was Sovereign for ten years, you see."

I turned in the water so quickly it sloshed against the sides of the tub and splashed to the floor. "No, I don't see. You keep all these secrets from me. How could I possibly have any idea?"

"It's just that Rebecca doesn't want to have anything to do with it, with the Acquisition. She can't."

"Why not?" This was the most Renee had told me about the Acquisition since she revealed the multiple trials. I needed her to keep talking.

She sank to the floor next to the tub, resting on the bath mat. "I don't see why I should keep it from you anymore, not now that you and Mr. Sinclair have…"

"Tell me."

"It's going to make everything so much worse for you." Tears welled in her eyes.

I was glad I hadn't told her about what we did that night in the library. She may have had a total come-apart.

"Rebecca found me at a time in my life when I had no purpose. I-I…" She examined her hands. "I was young and was selling my body in New Orleans." Red rose from her collar and flowed into her face.

"I'm not judging you, Renee." I had no right to pass judgment on anything anyone did to get by.

"Well, she found me there. Just happened across me, really. It was almost time for the Acquisition Ball, and the Vinemonts had been chosen that year. She was the eldest, so it fell to her to go through the process. I didn't realize it then, but she was desperate to find her Acquisition. I was it. I was desperate to get out of New Orleans. So, it was fate." The sorrow in her voice, the sense of betrayal, tore at me.

"I'm sorry, Renee."

"Oh, it was a long time ago." She swiped a tear away. "It was just that Rebecca was so kind and caring. And she truly was, even though the Acquisition was hanging over her head. Her maid at the time became my ally and told me how Rebecca had always been a lovely, sweet person. She was also a doting mother. I saw that myself. The way she loved on those boys of hers was beautiful."

She paused and took a deep breath. "And she was good to me, too. She really was, until she couldn't be anymore."

"The ball?"

Renee nodded and absentmindedly picked at her collar. "Yes, there and then Christmas." She blanched. "And then spring and summer."

"What happened, Renee? What happens at those trials?"

"It depends on the Sovereign. My year—" Her voice caught in her throat. "They say my year was one of the most brutal in Acquisition history. They say it with pride, like it was a feather in their cap to enjoy so much suffering."

Though the water was still warm, chills ran up and down my spine.

"Each trial has the same bent—in accordance with tradition—but the Sovereign can choose to add little twists to 'enhance' the experience. Christmas was the worst for me." Her dark eyes sought mine. They were haunted, immensely sad. "The worst for both of us, Rebecca and me. And now I'm afraid it'll be the worst for you, too."

"What happened at Christmas, Renee?" I needed to know but dreaded her answer.

"My year? My year, they chained us out in the cold. It was freezing. The three of us shivered and cried. Have you ever been truly cold, to the point where your skin goes numb, but underneath there are a million needle pricks?" Her voice took on a faraway tone, and I realized she was no longer looking at me. She was still chained, cold, and afraid.

"They sat in heated tents and watched, drinking, laughing, and giving in to their most basic desires while we suffered." She ran her hands up and down her arms. "Then, when they were ready for us, they brought us inside. We were on the verge of hypothermia. One of us even lost a toe from frostbite, though I heard that losing body parts was a rule violation. Everything in moderation." She laughed, high and desperate.

"They laid us out on the tables in their tents. I was glad to be in the warmth...and then I wasn't. They took turns. There were so many." A tremor shot through her.

Horror welled in me. Is that what Vinemont intended to do to me? Let me be raped by the masked ghouls from the ball?

"They hurt me. I can't lie. They did. But at some point during it, I sort of...disconnected. I was gone, burned away for the rest of the trial and for quite some time after. Rebecca wasn't so lucky. We had been, we were..."

I reached out and smoothed her hair away from her face with my damp hand. "It's okay, Renee. It's okay. I'm sorry."

I regretted reopening her wounds, but I needed to know. It was now or never.

She rubbed her tears away on her sleeve. "I loved her. I was certain she loved me. But that trial, what they did to me. It changed her, made her cold, hard. That's how they win. Do you understand? The only way to win is to become one of them, to *really* be the sort of monster that can rule the entire depraved aristocracy with an iron fist. Do you see? That's what they'll do to Mr. Sinclair. He'll fall. He'll break. But he'll win. And when he does..."

Her sad eyes captured mine, foretelling my own dark future by retelling her past. "Rebecca won, but she lost herself."

CHAPTER TWENTY
SINCLAIR

"I CAN'T DO anything about it, Lucius." I sank down into a chair in the study while Lucius paced around the room.

"I'm tired of the Sovereign taking such a huge cut," Lucius said. "We work our asses off—well at least I do while you're out playing public servant—and then fucking Cal comes in here and demands a goddamn ransom."

"You know we have to pay." I pinched the bridge of my nose. "We've been over this a million times."

Being Sovereign came with an untold number perks, the main one being a cut of all the income from the other ruling families. There was a yearly price and it was due within the month. Pay or suffer the consequences.

I was already dealing with far too many consequences to add non-payment to the list.

Lucius kicked the waste basket next to my desk. "We're working the fucking Brazilians to death and putting even more pressure on our already troubled relations with our Mexican producers. Sugar cane isn't as lucrative as it used to be. Even a fuckwit like Cal should be able to do the simple math."

"I'm aware. It doesn't matter. We have to pay Cal." I couldn't say it any other way. The facts were what they were.

He stopped pacing and stared out the window into the deepening night. "What else are we going to have to give him?"

"What do you mean?"

"You know what I mean, *who* I mean—Stella." He turned to me, giving me the same pissed off look he'd worn ever since he realized I was the oldest and, therefore, in charge of him.

"Stella is none of your concern. She's mine."

His eyes narrowed. "She doesn't have to be."

I stood, suddenly seething. Did he know? "What are you talking about?"

He crossed his arms over his chest, a self-satisfied grin on his face. "Mom told me some of the rules. She said if Stella chose me, I could take your place in the Acquisition."

Fuck.

I was bone tired after the long day with Stella. I had a short fuse and Lucius was doing his damnedest to light it. "Oh did she? Did she tell you the rest of the rules? Did she tell you what happens if you lose?"

"You don't get to be Sovereign." He shrugged. "So what? That's not a loss. We'd be in the same situation we're already in."

I hesitated on the verge of telling him the true penalty, the blood that would be required for us to keep our position. It was an exhausting secret, one that weighed more heavily on me every day. Maybe if I shared the burden, it wouldn't be so crushing. I opened my mouth to speak the lethal truth when Farns knocked and entered.

"What?" I snapped.

"We've had a call from the hospital in town. It seems Ms. Rousseau's father has taken ill. He is in intensive care. Her stepbrother has requested she come. I wasn't sure what you would like me to do with this news."

"I know what *I'd* like you to do." Stella entered behind Farns, her quiet steps masked by Lucius' and my argument. How long had she been listening?

"It's probably some sort of trick cooked up by your stepbrother," I said. "I forbid you to go." Surely, she realized it was nothing more than a desperate ruse? Transparent and dumb, just like her stepbrother.

She strode to me and stared into my eyes, my soul. "You can't forbid me from seeing my father in intensive care."

I gave Farns a look. He took the hint and backed into the hallway and closed the door.

"I can and I just did. Go back to your room." I wasn't letting her out of this house again, not after what had happened in the cabin earlier. She'd gotten to me, lanced through my rotten core and into the one piece of true heart I had left. I didn't even know it was there until she'd clawed her way in there, too. Goddamn her.

"I'm not going anywhere until I speak to my father." She kicked her chin up and put her hands on her hips.

Lucius walked up behind her. "Sin, it's her dad, maybe you should—"

"Maybe you should shut the fuck up, Lucius." Seeing them together, standing like a united front against me, finally lit the powder keg. I grabbed Stella's arm and ripped her away from him, pressing her back into my chest and putting my hand at her throat. She tried to scratch me, but I squeezed harder, cutting off her airway until she complied. I held Lucius' gaze the entire time.

"She's mine. All of this." I slid my hand down her side, around her thigh, and cupped her pussy like the piece of shit caveman I was. "It's all mine. So, back the fuck off."

Lucius glowered and tensed. "I've had it with your shit."

I held her fast, taunting him. "What, you want to fight me? Won't you be embarrassed when I kick the shit out of

187

you in front of your little crush here? Maybe then I'll fuck her while you're bleeding on the ground?"

Lucius raised his fists. "Let her go, and I'm going to knock your fucking teeth out."

A sharp pain in my ribs shocked me out of our stare down. Stella had managed to sneak in an elbow while Lucius had me distracted. She pulled away from me and darted to stand behind Lucius, her hand on his arm. I thought I was a powder keg before. Now I was a fucking black powder factory going up in a blaze of heat and sound. He reached back, put a possessive hand on her hip, and smirked at me.

"I just want to see my father. That's all. Please, Vinemont." Her plea, delivered behind my leering brother, pushed me far past my limit.

"You do? Are you sure?" I turned my back and went to my desk, digging for a certain sheaf of papers.

"Yes, I'm sure. Please, I'll come back. I promise. I just need to see him."

"I'll tell you what, Stella." Venom laced every word. "I want you to do a little light reading. Then tell me if you still want to see him. If you do, you can go and visit him. How about it?"

"Fine." She sounded relieved.

I laughed, the sound cruel and harsh even on my ears. I found the papers I was looking for and held them in my hand. She'd have to come to me.

"Hand them over," Lucius said.

"Go fuck yourself. Stella, come here."

She stepped out from behind him and tentatively approached me. She wasn't fearful, but she wasn't trusting, either. I gripped the papers tighter.

Lucius trailed his hand down her arm. I wanted to pummel his face until he was no longer capable of begging me to stop.

Her fear was back. I needed it. I ate it up. It reminded me of what I needed to do, what I *had* to do. Even so, it tore at my heart, leaving a part of me shredded and raw. I wanted to say I'd never hurt her. Never give her reason to fear me. But it would be a lie.

I passed her the papers and then held my hands up to show her I meant no harm. But I did. The papers were the dagger, her reading them would twist the blade deep into her back. She took them over to one of the sofas next to a bright lamp. Darkness had fallen outside, painting the grounds in somber gray tones.

She read the first page, then flipped to the second. I knew when she understood. I knew the exact moment when she read the words, when she flipped to the third page to see her father's signature.

"He sold you to me, Stella."

Her gaze rose to mine, horror shining in her eyes along with myriad other emotions—all black, all painful.

"Before you even came in that night, into the room where he and I sat, he'd already signed that contract in your hands. One million dollars. I was so pleased with my good fortune. That was a pittance for a woman like you. He eagerly agreed, signing the paper and sending you to me. He even told me how to phrase my offer to you before you came in. Very helpful, really. And it worked. Oh, how it worked. You came out to the car as planned. Then you came here, as planned. He knew you'd sacrifice yourself for him. The one man you thought loved you was actually the one man who sold you to me. And, just so you know, he was guilty of every single charge against him. I give you my word."

Her hand rose to her face, covering her mouth as she gasped for air. I hadn't hit her, hadn't touched her, but I knew as surely as she sat there that I'd destroyed some deep piece of her heart. It was blasted away, spoiled so that nothing could ever grow there again. Loathing rose in me—for myself, for her father, for everything.

She dropped the papers and stood, turning her back on me and staggering to the dark windows. Lucius rushed to her, steadying her by the shoulder. I could do nothing but wish him harm and wish her comfort. After all I'd done and all I would have to do, I still just wanted her to look at me again the way she had in the cabin. It was only hours ago, but now seemed like a lifetime.

I thought I'd seen love in her eyes, or something like it, as if I knew. I didn't know anything about that particular emotion, not really. But, I didn't remember anyone ever looking at me that way, with so much genuine feeling. It was guarded, but it was there. I wanted it back. I'd strangled any fledgling feelings she may have had with the documents that now lay on the floor, but I still wanted her. I wanted her to come to me for comfort, for support.

Lucius pulled her into his side as her sobs rose and fell. I willed her to leave him and come to me, to return to me and throw her arms around my shoulders. I would hold her while she cried. I would whisper sweet words into her ear. I would soothe her and bring her out of her despair.

My heart swelled, as if drunk on her tears. I could make it right. Somehow. I would try.

Her sobs stopped and her breathing slowed. She lifted her head, staring out into the inky gray of night.

I would tell her. I didn't care if Lucius heard. I was sorry, so fucking sorry.

"Stella—"

"I choose Lucius."

"What?" Her words were a jolt to my system—unbelievable, false. She couldn't mean it, not after what we'd been through, what we'd shared in the cabin.

She turned to me, her tear-streaked face bearing an expression that was a mix of heartbreak and hatred.

"I said I choose Lucius as my owner instead of you," she spat.

"You can't—"

"You heard her, Sin." Lucius wrapped his arm around her waist. "She chose me. She's mine now."

She stepped back from him, pushing his arm away in

disgust. "Don't touch me. Leave me alone, both of you."

She rushed through the room, running as if demons were at her heels. We both watched her go—one brother destroyed, and the other exhilarated.

She wouldn't look at me, though she was all I could see. She retreated down the hallway, disappearing from my view. My soul seemed to have left with her; my legs were no longer strong enough to hold up the empty shell of my body. I sank into the chair.

What have I done?

After a few moments of silence, a door slammed somewhere far away in the house. Her door.

The sound jarred Lucius into motion. He followed Stella's trail like a seasoned hunter, smooth and focused.

I wanted to stop him, to work the same violence on him that I had on Stella's heart.

"Leave her alone, Lucius." Though my soul was gone, my rage still burned.

He glanced over his shoulder, triumphant and vicious. "She's mine now. I know the rules. I call the shots, and I have no intentions of ever leaving her alone."

"I will fucking end you." I forced myself to move and followed him into the hall.

He flipped me off and took the stairs two at a time.

"Game on, big brother."

THE ACQUISITION SERIES

Available Now

MAGNATE, Acquisition Series Book 2

LUCIUS VINEMONT SPIRITED me away to a world of sugar cane and sun. There is nothing he cannot give me on his lavish Cuban plantation. Each gift seduces me, each touch seals my fate. There is no more talk of depraved competitions or his older brother – the one who'd stolen me, claimed me, and made me feel things I never should have. Even as Lucius works to make me forget Sinclair, my thoughts stray back to him, to the dark blue eyes that haunt my sweetest dreams and bitterest nightmares. Just like every dream, this one must end. Christmas will soon be here, and with it, the second trial of the Acquisition.

SOVEREIGN, Acquisition Series Book 3

THE ACQUISITION HAS ruled my life, ruled my every waking moment since Sinclair Vinemont first showed up at my house offering an infernal bargain to save my father's life. Now I know the stakes. The charade is at an end, and Sinclair has far more to lose than I ever did. But this knowledge hasn't strengthened me. Instead, each revelation breaks me down until nothing is left but my fight and my rage. As I struggle to survive, only one question remains. How far will I go to save those I love and burn the Acquisition to the ground?

EROTICA TITLES BY CELIA AARON

Forced by the Kingpin
Forced Series, Book 1

I've been on the trail of the local mob kingpin for months. I know his haunts, habits, and vices. The only thing I didn't know was how obsessed he was with me. Now, caught in his trap, I'm about to find out how far he and his local cop-on-the-take will go to keep me silent.

Forced by the Professor
Forced Series, Book 2

I've been in Professor Stevens' class for a semester. He's brilliant, severe, and hot as hell. I haven't been particularly attentive, prepared, or timely, but he hasn't said anything to me about it. I figure he must not mind and intends to let me slide. At least I thought that was the case until he told me to stay after class today. Maybe he'll let me off with a warning?

Forced by the Hitmen
Forced Series, Book 3

I stayed out of my father's business. His dirty money never mattered to me, so long as my trust fund was full of it. But now I've been kidnapped by his enemies and stuffed in a bag. The rough men who took me have promised to hurt me if I make a sound or try to run. I know, deep down, they are going to hurt me no matter what I do. Now I'm cuffed to their bed. Will I ever see the light of day again?

Forced by the Stepbrother
Forced Series, Book 4

Dancing for strange men was the biggest turn on I'd ever known. Until I met him. He was able to control me, make me hot, make me need him, with nothing more than a look. But he was a fantasy. Just another client who worked me up and paid my bills. Until he found me, the real me. Now, he's backed me into a corner. His threats and promises, darkly whispered in tones of sex and violence, have bound me surer than the cruelest ropes. At first I was unsure, but now I know – him being my stepbrother is the least of my worries.

Forced by the Quarterback
Forced Series, Book 5

For three years, I'd lusted after Jericho, my brother's best friend and quarterback of our college football team. He's never paid me any attention, considering me nothing more than a little sister he never had. Now, I'm starting freshman year and I'm sharing a suite with my brother. Jericho is over all the time, but he'll never see me as anything other than the shy girl he met three years ago. But that's not who I am. Not really. To get over Jericho – and to finally get off – I've arranged a meeting with HardcoreDom. If I can't have Jericho, I'll give myself to a man who will master me, force me, and dominate me the way I desperately need.

***

A Stepbrother for Christmas
The Hard and Dirty Holidays

Annalise dreads seeing her stepbrother at her family's Christmas get-together. Niles had always been so nasty, tormenting her in high school after their parents had gotten married. British and snobby, Niles did everything he could to hurt Annalise when they were younger. Now, Annalise hasn't seen Niles in three years; he's been away at school in England and Annalise has started her pre-med program in Dallas. When they reconnect, dark memories threaten, sparks fly, and they give true meaning to the "hard and dirty holidays."

Bad Boy Valentine
The Hard and Dirty Holidays

Jess has always been shy. Keeping her head down and staying out of sight have served her well, especially when a sexy photographer moves in across the hall from her. Michael has a budding career, a dark past, and enough ink and piercings to make Jess' mouth water. She is well equipped to watched him through her peephole and stalk him on social media. But what happens when the bad boy next door comes knocking?

Bad Boy Valentine Wedding
The Hard and Dirty Holidays

Jess and Michael have been engaged for three years, waiting patiently for Jess to finish law school before taking the next step in their relationship. As the wedding date approaches, their dedication to each other only grows, but outside forces seek to tear them apart. The bad boy will have to fight to keep his bride and Jess will have to trust him with her whole heart to make their happy ending a reality.

F*ck of the Irish
The Hard and Dirty Holidays

Eamon is my crush, the one guy I can't stop thinking about. His Irish accent, toned body, and sparkling eyes captivated me the second I saw him. But since he slept with my roommate, who claims she still loves him, he's been off limits. Despite my prohibition on dating him, he has other other ideas. Resisting him is the key to keeping my roommate happy, but giving in may bring me more pleasure than I ever imagined.

***

Zeus
Taken by Olympus, Book 1

One minute I'm looking after an injured gelding, the next I'm tied to a luxurious bed. I never believed in fairy tales, never gave a second thought to myths. Now that I've been kidnapped by a man with golden eyes and a body that makes my mouth water, I'm not sure what I believe anymore. . . But I know what I want.

<u>About the Author</u>

Celia Aaron is the self-publishing pseudonym of a published romance and erotica author. She loves to write stories with hot heroes and heroines that are twisty and often dark. Thanks for reading.